IN MEMORY OF

George Tony Starkovich

April 27, 1922 to February 26, 2014

He was called "The most contemptuous witness to ever come before the House Un-American Activities Committee."

George was a union organizer, war hero in WWII, the emcee at the International Youth Peace Rally (1950) during the Paul Robeson concert, and a life long fighter for civil rights and women's rights.

BLACKLISTED

A Family Targeted by McCarthy

G. A. Davis

COPYRIGHT

dvs publishing
2824 Winthrop Avenue
San Ramon, Ca   94538
dvspublishing@aol.com

Blacklisted
A Family Targeted by McCarthy

Cover art and design by Audrey Ann Davis
Model for cover photo: Zoe Davis-Watkins
Interior design by Audrey Ann Davis

Printed in the United States
ISBN 978-0-9883006-8-2

Acknowledgments

Many, many thanks to my family: Audrey, Adrienne, Faith, Kai, Rasheeda, Richard, Rick and Rickki Davis; Caroljo and Andrea Gibson; and Vickie Knight. A special thank you to Carol Emerson, Gayle Lopez, Susan Lyon, Nancy Mendenhall, Wayne Neal, Elaine Starkman, Marisa Samuels, Donna Van Sant, Wendell Watkins and Bonnie Weiss for your time, suggestions and invaluable help. I am also indebted to the SF writing group from Donna Levine's class on novel writing; Elaine Starkman's Memoir class, and the Antioch Senior Center writers group.

I wish to give special credit to my great granddaughter, Zoe Davis-Watkins for capturing the spirit of Josie, the main character in the book. We looked at hundreds of photos of teens but could not find the "look" we wanted. Her picture on the cover conveys the "serious and searching" young person we felt the character Josie and many of today's young people embody. At thirteen years old Zoe is a consummate actress. Thank you, Zoe, for a marvelous job.

G. A. Davis 2014

INTRODUCTION

The most well-known investigations by Joe McCarthy and the House Un-American Activities Committee were the hearings of the Hollywood Ten, resulting in the blacklisting of famous actors and screen writers. Not so well-known were the thousands of ordinary folk who were blacklisted and fired from their jobs during the McCarthy era. The FBI director, J. Edgar Hoover, had an army under his command dedicated to investigating radicals and liberals. The use of blacklisting was so prevalent that a right wing cottage industry flourished for the purpose of selling names to employers of militant individuals or possible organizers. Tens of thousands of people were investigated.

The story Blacklisted: A Family Targeted by McCarthy is a fictional account of an ordinary family and how they fought back. In real life there were countless struggles of working folk resisting intimidation and fighting for justice.

Many people, places and events in Blacklisted were used to create a feeling for the period and do not necessarily follow an accurate time line. Please see additional notes and definitions at the end of the story.

Gretchen A. Davis

DEDICATED TO
THE NEW PEOPLE;
THE YOUNG PEOPLE
WHO ARE INDEPENDENT,
ANTI-RACIST, AND QUESTION EVERYTHING.

BLACKLISTED

A Family Targeted by McCarthy

Chapter One

Mom and I'd lived with Aunt Celeste and Uncle Victor for only a few weeks when a brand new '54 Chevy began parking across the street from our house. There were two men in the car; I knew they were FBI agents. One morning they knocked on our door.

"I'm Agent Brock," said a man with beady eyes peering out from under his hat; he glanced here and there, never focusing on one thing.

"This is Agent Swacker." He nodded his head toward his partner. Both wore blue slacks and matching sports jackets. Agent Swacker smiled, but it wasn't a friendly smile. I felt a shiver go through me.

"Josie, get Victor," Aunt Celeste said. "Tell him the Feds are here." She closed the door making them wait outside until I came back with my uncle.

Uncle Victor walked slowly to the door.

"We'd like to ask you a few questions," Agent Brock told him. He showed his badge and held up his I.D. with a photograph on it. When he did, his coat opened and I saw a gun under his jacket. My insides started to churn.

Uncle Victor looked at the identification. He ran his fingers through thinning brown hair, smoothing it into place. The large round glasses he wore that made him look like an owl slid down his nose. "I don't have anything to say to you."

Brock handed Uncle Victor his card. "You can reach me at this number if you change your mind. If you're smart, you will."

"We'd like to help you," Agent Swacker, added. His smile grew bigger, but even less friendly.

"Not interested," Uncle Victor answered, returning the card, and shutting the door.

"Be smart," Brock shouted through the door. "Cooperate. It'll go better for your family."

My uncle jerked the door back open. "Are you threatening me?"

The two agents had started down the steps. Brock threw his arms up in the air, but didn't turn back. I must have looked worried because Uncle Victor put his arms around me.

"It's okay, Josie, it's scare tactics. The hearings start soon."

"They don't scare me," I said, with way more bravery than I felt.

"Good girl." He gave me a hug.

"They're back in their car," Aunt Celeste said, watching them through the window.

"Brock and Swacker," Uncle Victor said. "Sounds like a vaudeville act." He laughed.

I didn't think it was funny. Uncle Victor had been subpoenaed to appear before a Senate committee. It was called the House Committee on Un-American Activities. Aunt Celeste called the hearings a witch-hunt.

My uncle worked for a waterfront union in Seattle. His job was to meet with the ship owners and "walking bosses" when the workers had a beef about the contract or if the work wasn't safe. The House Committee said there were Communists in the union and they expected my uncle to tell them about his members and his political beliefs.

Naming names had become a well-known saying about Hollywood. Naming names meant being a stool-pigeon. If a movie star refused to implicate others as Communists or Communist sympathizers, he was black-listed; or if they "took the fifth" and refused to testify against themselves, the black-list was automatic.

Mom, Aunt C and Uncle Victor didn't talk much about what might happen at the hearings. I noticed Aunt C's hands were slightly shaking after the two agents left. I was afraid my uncle might be sent to jail if he didn't answer their questions.

Each morning the two agents arrived and parked under the madrona tree across from our house. They stayed there until Uncle Victor left for work; then they followed him. They became part of the landscape. Sometimes I even forgot they were there.

⚖ ⚖ ⚖

It was always hard for me to get up in the morning, especially when it rained. The sound of rain on the roof or windowpane would lull me back to sleep in a second. I woke up with Aunt C calling me. She must have called several times because she sounded cross.

"Breakfast's ready. Miss Josephine Brown Thompson, your food's getting cold!"

I climbed from underneath warm covers and dressed in a pleated skirt, sweater and tan saddle shoes.

On the way downstairs, I stopped on the landing where our family pictures hung on the wall. I blew a kiss at the photograph of my Dad. I never knew him, but he looked like a swell guy standing there with Uncle Victor, arms around shoulders. I was only three months old when Dad was killed in the war in Spain. He was one of the volunteers who went to stop fascists before the Second World War broke out. He was in the Abraham Lincoln Brigade, men and women from the United States.

I winked at the picture of Uncle Victor. All over Seattle I met people who knew him. Sometimes a total stranger would stop me and ask, "Aren't you Victor Jenkins' niece?" They would introduce themselves and ask me to give him their best.

When I got downstairs Uncle Victor was talking on the phone.

"Morning, Unc."

He covered the speaker with his hand and mouthed, "Morning." I wondered who he was talking to that was so important. If he was on the phone when I came downstairs he usually asked the party to wait while he greeted me. This time he kept listening and gave me a smile.

He spent a lot of time on the telephone, writing leaflets and going to meetings.

When the picture On The Waterfront came out some kids at school thought unions were nothing but a bunch of gangsters. Uncle Victor says there are some gangster bosses in a few unions, like Dave Beck, the head of the Teamsters. But the stories he told me about people who organized the unions were heroes. We wouldn't have an eight-hour day, overtime pay or sick pay, if it wasn't for them. Many men and women died organizing the unions. Not that they ever taught that history in school.

Mom was already at her job at Goody's Bakery. She left for work at 3:00 a.m. to get bread and pastry ready for customers. I hated it that she worked so hard. She had a cough from the flour that they called the "baker's cough." I heard there were many diseases named after the kind of work people did, like miner's lung. I wondered if there was one called high school student's scrambled brain. I bet you could get that from too much unrelated information and myths like "Columbus discovered America" or "the Pilgrims settled the New World," as if there were no one else here before they arrived. No one ever mentioned that Columbus was a slave trader. One time I brought up in class Hispaniola, and the death of thousands of Indians Columbus and his men enslaved. The teacher told me, "Oh, I don't think that is true, dear." Then she moved on to dates we should memorize.

⚖ ⚖ ⚖

Breakfast was waiting for me on the yellow Formica table. Aunt C had fixed my favorites: over-easy eggs, fried potatoes and ham.

"Morning, Aunt C. Who's Uncle Victor talking to?"

"Not sure," she answered from the back porch off the kitchen. The room doubled as a laundry room and her studio. She had fixed breakfast and was already working on a large painting. My Aunt C was the most beautiful woman in our family, even dressed in her old plaid shirt and jeans she wore when she painted. Her hair was turning gray, making startling streaks in her coal black hair. She had flair. An article in *Photoplay Magazine* said the movie star Katherine Hepburn had flair, and so did Aunt C. She wore clothes that were different, peasant blouses with shades of turquoise and chartreuse. She put her hair up in a bun and stuck a chopstick in her hair. Once she told me she got away with dressing differently because people expect artists to be different, even if they weren't.

"Uncle Victor looked real serious," I told her, still curious about the phone call.

"The phone started ringing at a God-awful hour. He's been on it ever since," she answered.

"Mmmm, breakfast looks good."

"Would you ask Victor if he wants breakfast? He needs to get off the phone."

⚖️ ⚖️ ⚖️

Uncle Victor wanted breakfast; he always did. I'd never known him to leave the house without breakfast, no matter what.

While he ate, Aunt Celeste poured herself a cup of coffee, and lit a cigarette. "Victor, honey, you were on the phone a long time."

He fanned away the smoke from her cigarette.

"Oh, sorry," she said, snubbing the cigarette out in the ashtray.

He didn't smoke, and for that matter he didn't drink, or swear. He was the opposite of Aunt C.

"Someone broke into the union hall last night," Uncle Victor announced. "One of the guys said it looked like they were after our records—not that there's anything to find. They smashed up my office and broke a lot of windows."

"That's terrible! Who do you think did it?" I asked.

"Probably the Feds, or they arranged it. It looks like harassment because the hearings are starting soon. It was an inside job. None of the doors or locks were forced."

Uncle Victor never got rattled. He talked about the break-in like it was a lab experiment, weighing all the facts.

"Maybe the Feds got the keys from the owners," he continued, "or they found out who we use as a locksmith. Perhaps we have a spy in the union."

"Any suspects Uncle Victor?"

"A couple, but no solid proof."

"Like who? Anybody I know?"

"Josie, honey, I can't say. It's not right to accuse someone without proof."

"The Committee does it all the time!" I argued. "They accuse people without proof. Sometimes they lie."

"This business with The Committee, it isn't about right or wrong. It's about breaking the trade unions."

"Do you think they could break your union, Uncle Victor?"

"The Committee smears us and frightens people. Laws like the Taft-Hartley Act make it tough to defend our members. If we take direct action, like walk off the job, we can go to jail."

"But could the hearings wreck your union?"

"We're solid now, but the employers will keep coming after us. They'd like everyone to go back to working eighteen hours a day, seven days a week."

We spent a lot of time at the union hall. There were parties and dances; whole families brought their kids. When it got late, the little kids were put to sleep on blankets on the floor. There was lots of food. I learned all kinds of dances, like the camel walk and hustle from members from the east coast and the schottische and the polka from older Scandinavian members.

The union had a lending library in the hall. Sometimes I went there after school, and during summer vacation. That's where I read *Freedom Road*, *Two Years before the Mast* and short stories by O. Henry.

"Can I go with you and Uncle Victor to clean up?

"Don't you have school?"

"Not until the afternoon when I have a test."

"Did you study?"

"Yep."

"You always do well." Aunt C smiled.

"Maybe not." It was confession time. "I kinda got into it with my history teacher."

Aunt C's eyebrows went up. "Kinda got into it?" she asked.

"I asked the teacher about Spartacus, why we never learn about things like the slave revolts; those cats almost brought down Rome! Real snotty like, she asks me if I'd like to teach the class?"

Aunt C sighed, "You know, some people can't stand young people challenging them."

"Seems like a history teacher would know better."

"Seems like," she agreed.

"Well," Uncle Victor said, "there's an old saying, If you're going to dance you have to pay the fiddler."

"They can fiddle all they want, for all I care! After class the teacher grilled me. She asked me where I got my ideas."

Aunt C groaned, "You want me or your Mom to talk to her?"

"Nah, Mom's working all the time. Besides the whole thing is just stupid." I looked over at Uncle Victor who had a big grin on his face.

"Celeste, maybe we should go help the teacher," he suggested. "She might need some protection from Josie."

Uncle Victor was still smiling. I think he was kind of proud of me for speaking up. He had a way of making me feel I could do anything when I set my mind to it.

"So can I go with you to clean up the hall?"

"We can use all the help we can get," Uncle Victor said, still smiling.

⚖ ⚖ ⚖

Uncle Victor went to talk on the phone again and Aunt C poured herself another coffee. I noticed she had dark circles under her eyes.

"You look tired."

"I couldn't sleep. I had the dream again."

"About being chased?"

"Always, the same one. I felt like I was running all night."

"Are you worried about the agents who visited?"

"I try not to, but it's hard when they watch the house every day."

"They're so dumb."

"What do you mean?"

"They have a brand new car, and it's so ratty. You should see what it looks like inside."

"How do you know?"

She frowned, so I explained. "A bunch of us kids were walking home from school and the agents had the car doors open. They looked for something inside. You could see everything. It was nasty: old paper coffee cups, sandwich bags, crumpled newspapers - like a pig pen."

"Be careful," she said. She shook her head in disgust.

"That agent - the one I know now is called Brock - he jumped up and yelled at us, "What the hell are you looking at?" Then he used the F word. "Get the eff out of here!" We all started snickering until he put his hand under his jacket and stepped toward us.

Chapter Two

Aunt C warmed up the car's engine and I tried to get comfortable in the back seat. The seats were old and hard. I squiggled around, but nothing worked. Uncle Victor fiddled with the dials on the radio. A familiar voice came on. "This is B. Buck Butterball Ritchie, transmitting to you from the toe of the Hood's Canal...."

"Turn on some good music, not that cowboy stuff," I pleaded.

"I'm trying to find the news," Uncle Victor said.

We were the only people I knew that drove a Willys. Uncle Victor said it was made by the same company that made Jeeps during World War Two. The car was old but ran well, although it was embarrassing when he honked the horn. The beep, beep, sounded like a baby chicken.

Uncle Victor was a good mechanic. Ever since I was a little kid I was his number one helper; that's how I learned the names of the tools. But the neatest thing was driving around, just me and him. We talked about politics, science and how things worked. Lots of times when I didn't understand something, he would say, "Just think about it, use your logic."

Aunt C backed the Willys out of the driveway and we pulled alongside the green Chevrolet. When I looked out of the window I found myself eyeball to eyeball with Agent Brock. I gave him a smile. Then I couldn't help myself, my thumb went right to my nose and I gave the jackass the five-fingered salute. He looked disappointed. Can that idiot possibly think I'm friendly?

"Stop that?" Aunt C snapped. "Don't play with those people."

"I wouldn't think of it!" In a pig's eye. I spent the rest of the trip thinking of ways to irritate the FBI agents. I didn't think there was much I could do, but it was fun to dream.

⚖ ⚖ ⚖

When we got to the hall, several men were waiting for Uncle Victor at the entrance, so we let him out and went to find a parking space. Aunt C pulled into a spot in front of the totem pole in Pioneer Square. This one was my favorite. It had blue color, something you didn't see a lot; most of the poles were black and red. I felt bad that the pole was starting to rot and the colors were fading. Businessmen from Seattle stole it from Alaskan natives in the 1800s and gave it to the city for a landmark. The city fathers didn't take care of the pole. I mentioned it to Uncle Victor, and he said, "It's typical of big shots - they take what they want and when it's served its purpose they throw it on the junk heap; just like they do to people if they don't fight back."

⚖ ⚖ ⚖

When we reached the union hall, the doors to the main meeting room were open and it looked like someone had thrown a bomb into the place. A ton of broken glass was on the floor, stuffing and springs poked out of a sofa and dark marks dotted the upholstery like someone had tried to burn it. I sniffed a smell of what I thought was lighter fluid. A large metal coffee pot with a big dent in its side sat on a pile of coffee grounds; cups and saucers lay in pieces around it. The door to Uncle Victor's office was torn off the hinges and filing cabinets lay one on top of another like fallen dominoes.

"Wow," I said.

Aunt C swore under her breath.

We waved to Uncle Victor sitting with a number of men at the far end of the hall.

Goldie, the president of the union left the meeting and came to meet us. Goldie had reddish brown skin, and wore his thick curly hair short. You might have thought he was a business man, or professor, because he wore slacks with razor sharp creases, white shirt and corduroy jacket. That is, you might have thought that except for the gold earring in his left ear.

"We came to help," Aunt C told him.

"Me too," I said.

"Thanks, it's a real mess. Maybe you could help the old man who runs the library."

Before I could answer, Aunt C took off to work on Uncle Victor's wrecked office, so I had a chance to bug Goldie. Whenever I ran into him, which was pretty often because he was sweet on my Mom, I asked him something about pirates. We had sort of made a game of it. When I first asked about the gold earring, he replied, "Because I'm a pirate, arrgh!!!" I asked a couple more times, but got the same answer. Then I started asking him, "How's the looting and pillaging going?" And he would answer, "Doing well, Jean Lefitte, at your service, Ma'am." I learned a lot about pirates. One day he said he was Ching Shih and told me to look it up if I didn't recognize the name. She was a female pirate in the 1800s. Goldie said pirates were bad guys, but didn't hold a candle to modern day ones, like the employers and their henchmen, The Committee and the FBI.

I liked him okay as a person, but I wasn't too happy about his liking Mom. And nobody could replace my dad. Besides, I had Uncle Victor.

I found the old man busy putting books back on shelves. Piles of books were on the floor and some were torn beyond repair. The old fellow carried a big load of books and was dripping sweat and breathing hard.

"Boy, they sure tore things up," I remarked.

"Sons of bitches," the old man snarled. "Oh, sorry, Miss Josie."

"It's okay. Can you use some help?"

"Appreciate it."

While putting books back on the shelves, I found some I had read, *Two Years Before the Mast*, and O. Henry's Short Stories.

"Who do you think did this?" I asked.

"Some rats," the old man answered.

"Think it was an inside job?"

"Lots of people don't like the union."

"Like who?"

"Employers, finks, the Feds. Who knows?"

"Best guess, who would it be?"

He looked me dead in the eye, "Loose lips sink ships."

I could take a hint. The tone of his voice told me that was his final answer and don't ask again.

We had most of the books back on the shelves in record time. The last few were badly damaged, so the old man told me to dump them in the garbage can by the kitchen door. I put the torn-up books in the trash and headed back to gather my things up for school.

I started toward the main meeting room and almost ran into a man dressed in a suit. It was Agent Brock, the one I had given the five-fingered salute. He stared at the men gathered at the far end of the hall and made notes on a small notepad. He looked up at me, but neither of us spoke. He tipped his hat and winked. All the time he had a little smirk on his face. Then he hurried down the stairs.

Uncle Victor appeared. "Who was that?" he asked.

"Give you a hint, Uncle Victor: green car, every day, front of the house."

"Hmmm," was all he said.

"What do you think he wanted?"

"He's letting us know what a big man he is."

"Boy, that takes a lot of nerve, coming in here."

"Not so much," Uncle Victor said. "He's got the Feds, the US Army and the police on his side...."

"Still," I argued, "You going to do anything about it?"

"Keep doing our job," he answered.

"Like?"

"Like we always do: take action, organize, defend our brothers and sisters."

⚖ ⚖ ⚖

I got to Garfield High School in plenty of time to take my history test. I did okay, even though my mind wasn't a hundred percent on it. There were so many things to think about.

I never told Aunt C, Uncle Victor or Mom that I saw the two FBI agents at school right before my history teacher tried to pump me about my ideas and ask me questions about Uncle Victor. There wasn't any point in telling the family about it; they had enough on their minds. Besides, I could take care of myself.

Chapter Three

I got up early. It was the weekend and there were a lot of things I wanted to do like going to Kress's Five and Dime Store to buy records. The dime store and Bob Summerize's record shop were the only two places you could buy Rhythm and Blues records. At Kress's they were in a separate section away from the other records. Mostly it was the Negro kids at Garfield that played Rhythm and Blues at house parties. You couldn't hear it on the radio except Bob Summerize, a Negro disc jockey who came on at eleven at night—way too late for me on a school night.

I was surprised to find Mom in the kitchen drinking coffee.

She was still in her bathrobe, but her hair was brushed and pinned up. My Aunt C was the prettiest woman in the family, but Mom was no slouch. Her eyes were the same shade as her hair, pecan. Mom had dark black eyebrows. Her eyelashes looked like she wore make up, which she never did. Her eyes always told you what kind of mood she was in: gold flecks like sunshine when she was happy, purple when she was worried. That morning they were purple.

13

"What's going on?" I asked. "Where's Aunt C and Uncle Victor?"

"Victor's at the union office, and your aunt went to the Graphic Arts Studio."

"This early?"

"It's an emergency. Hector Caceres was arrested last night. Victor is getting his members together to raise money and your aunt and other artists are making signs and printing leaflets."

"Can I help? I helped Aunt C before." I had worked with her many times when she silk screened posters. There was a lot involved because the paint had to dry before the signs could be stacked together. Ropes were strung up like clothes lines and the wet signs hung on them with clothes pins until they dried.

"They could use your help, but not with the signs. Hector has a little girl, ten years old. Her mother died years ago. He needs someone to stay with her until the union can get him released from jail. Someone who won't panic if the Feds come around."

"Yes! Anything to help."

Mom smiled. "Victor said you would. The Cannery Workers Union will pay you."

"I don't want their money."

"Victor said you would say that. They insisted."

"It's my contribution. I won't take any money."

Mom didn't say anything. She smiled at me the way Uncle Victor does when he's proud of me.

"You know, Hector Caceres is a very respected man."

I knew what she meant. Everybody thought he was one of the bravest men. He became president of his union after the president and vice president before him were murdered by an employer.

We walked together from E. Fir Street over to Jackson Street. I took the bus to Beacon Hill, where the Caseres family lived and Mom took one going downtown to the Cannery Workers Building. The Graphic Arts Studio was in their building, and she went to help with the printing

When the bus passed the Marine Hospital I looked for the giant crack in the ground made by the earthquake in 1949. I always looked for it even if it gave me a shiver. Old Mom Nature could be pretty scary. They said it was the biggest one since ancient times. The KJR Radio Station antennae fell down and over a thousand brick walls collapsed in Seattle.

I got off a few blocks past the hospital and checked the paper Mom had given me with the Caceres family's address. I wondered if Anthony Avilá, another one of the leaders in the Cannery Workers would be around. He was the most handsome and sexiest guy. I found the address. It was a corner house with a tower on it. The paint was peeling off the house and the grass was tall. I guessed they had stuff to think about other than making things neat. The doorbell didn't work so I knocked loudly. It was dark inside and looked empty. I knocked again and finally heard footsteps coming from way inside the house. Finally a short, handsome man opened the door.

"I'm Josie," I said, my heart doing a pitty-pat as he gave me a friendly smile.

"Anthony Avilá," he said extending his hand. "Victor said you were coming."

I laughed to myself. Uncle Victor had told them I'd sit before I had said yes.

"Maria isn't up yet."

He led me to the back of the house. There wasn't much furniture in the living room or dining room. The kitchen at the back of the house was big, with a large wooden table in the center of the room and lots of chairs, none of which matched. The table had nicks and scratches but was clean. A woman sat at the table eating. Her smile revealed brown teeth, many of them missing. She had stringy hair and wore a flower over one ear. She made me think of someone who might be more at home sitting on a stool in a tavern than in the home of a union leader.

"Can I fix you breakfast?" Anthony asked. "I'm a good cook."

"No. Thanks, I already ate."

When he and the bar babe finished their food, he said he had to go to the union hall and would be back in the afternoon. Before he left he gave me the number at the hall, in case I needed to get in touch with him. When they were gone he had me lock the front door, explaining the agents who arrested Mr. Caceres came in when the door wasn't locked. They came to his bed while he was sleeping and woke Maria down the hall, scaring her. Anthony said to let her sleep as long as possible.

I made myself at home, looking through the records by the phonograph player in the front room. There were only a few old 78s and a couple of 33 and 1/3s I'd never heard of, and most were in a different language, except for one, *The Little Grass Shack in Kealakekua Hawaii*, which was in English.

Since there wasn't much to do I found a broom and swept the front room and dining room. It was pretty easy since there was little furniture. When that was done I went to the kitchen and warmed up some left over coffee. Mom didn't like me to drink coffee. She said "It'll stunt your growth." But I was so tall I drank as much of it as I could.

In the middle of my second cup I heard soft footsteps and a little girl appeared. She wore a nightie and slippers and her dark hair hung down to the middle of her back. She was prettier than I expected, but short for a ten-year-old. She had nut brown skin, rosy cheeks and raisin eyes. She smiled the tiniest smile.

"Maria?"

She nodded yes, but looked worried.

"My name is Josie. Your dad asked me to babysit."

"I know." Her frown disappeared and she smiled again.

I told her there was food on the stove. She took the plate that Anthony had left for her and sat down to eat. I made a search for silverware and found a drawer full, all mismatched. So were the plates, cups and saucers.

While she ate I tried to think of questions to get to know her, but she would only answer yes, no, or shake her head. Finally, after a long silence she asked me if I wanted to see her room, and she led me upstairs. The bottom floor of the house was almost bare, but starting with the stairs everything came alive. The steps were stained, varnished and polished. The wood trim and floor in the upper hall shone; there was bright flowered wallpaper on the walls.

Maria took me to her room at the end of the hallway. Inside, the color popped out, all baby blue and pink. There was a canopy over her bed and a ton of ruffles.

"Would you like to see my collection?" She showed me a small dresser in the corner of the room. A mirror was attached to the dresser and another lay on the tabletop. I could see this wasn't for doing makeup, but to show off her collection of glass animals and figurines. The glass shimmered in the light and reflected in the mirrors.

"Maria, these are beautiful!"

She gave me a big smile.

"Papa got them for me."

We stood looking at them and then she asked, "Do you want to see my pictures?" She brought two photographs, one of a man and woman together and one of the woman by herself. The pictures had turned brown with age. The couple looked old-fashioned, dressed in formal clothing, staring stiffly into the camera.

"Your mom and dad?"

"My Mama," she said. "It's the only pictures I have of her." She smiled, but looked sad.

I remembered Mom said her mother had died.

I saw a grass skirt hanging on the wall and asked her about it. She brightened up, telling me she took hula lessons. "My mom was from Hawaii. Do you want to see me dance?" she asked.

We headed downstairs to the record player in the front room. She put on *The Little Grass Shack*. When the music started she tapped her feet, getting the timing. Then, out of the corner of my eye I noticed someone passing by the window. The yard alongside the house sloped down, but I could see the top of a man's hat through the window.

"Just a sec," I told Maria. I made a quick check of the front door and saw a car parked across the street with several men in it. My stomach churned. I remembered the back door and wondered if it was locked.

Maria, why don't you go up and get your grass skirt. It'd be neat to see you dance in it."

"Okay," she said, heading upstairs. I ran as fast as I could through the kitchen to the back door. I slid the bolt closed and pulled down the shade just as I heard someone coming up the back steps. I made it to the front room as Maria returned, wearing the grass skirt over her pajamas.

"Start the record again," I suggested.

The music began and she started swaying, arms and hands moving like gentle ocean waves on a quiet day.

We were interrupted by a loud knock at the front door. "Keep dancing," I said, "It's probably a stupid salesman."

I raised the blind and there were two men wearing suits standing on the porch. One of them held up a badge. I thought about the men they were trying to deport, like Maria's father. If her Papa got sent to the Philippines, would he be put in jail or even killed? I knew his union supported the peasant uprising. Now I understood why Aunt C kept telling me not to play around with these guys. This wasn't a game.

I opened the door a crack with the chain still on, and in my most grown-up voice asked, "May I help you?"

17

The agent told me his name and showed me his identification. "We'd like to speak to the girl," he said.

"What girl?"

"The Caceres girl." He sneered.

"Do you have a warrant?"

"It's not like that, we just want to ask her a few questions."

"No thank you," I told him. I closed the door and pulled down the shade.

"Open the door," he demanded.

I could hear him swearing all the way down the steps.

Maria was still dancing. "Was it a salesman?"

"It wasn't important. Show me how you do that thing with your hands. But first I have to make a phone call." I called the Graphic Arts Studio and told Mom about the visitors. Terry told me to sit tight; Goldie was only a few blocks away. She said she would tell Anthony Avilá about the visit.

Maria showed me how each hand movement meant something and she sang a song in Hawaiian. By the time she finished Goldie knocked on the door.

"Heard you had visitors," he said, and then he spotted Maria. "Why hello there. What's your name?"

I introduced Maria to Goldie.

She stared at him. Finally she asked, "Why do you wear an earring?"

Goldie and I burst out laughing.

"He used to be a pirate," I answered, "but he's retired."

"You aren't afraid of me, are you?" Goldie asked.

Marie shook her head, and smiled at him. Before she could ask him more questions, Anthony Avilá and his lady friend appeared. Her hair was stringier, and the flower had wilted, but I was glad to see both of them.

⚖ ⚖ ⚖

We drove home in Goldie's car, an old Franklin, which was even older than Uncle Victor's. The window on his side wouldn't roll up all the way and the inside of the car smelled like oil.

"I don't know about you and Uncle Victor. What's with driving these old heaps?"

"Easy to repair. I'm planning on keeping her until I can't get parts anymore."

"Why do guys always refer to their cars as she, or her?"

"Josie, are you okay? What did the feds want?"

I told him the whole story.

"Good girl," he said. "I knew they picked the right person for the job."

The rest of the drive, he asked me about school, how I was getting along at Garfield. For once I was really glad to see him.

⚖ ⚖ ⚖

The next day we got a phone call from Mr. Caceres, and he asked to speak to me. He thanked me for babysitting and donating the money to the union.

"Maria really liked you," he said. "Please come and visit us." Then he talked to Uncle Victor.

When Uncle Victor got off the phone he told me more members of the Cannery Workers Union had been arrested, thirty-five all together.

⚖ ⚖ ⚖

A few days after babysitting, I came home from school to find Mom there, so I had a chance to ask her about something that was bothering me. Why would a guy like Anthony Avilá, a union leader everybody respected, pal around with a woman who seemed so uncool.

Mom told me, "You can't tell anything about someone by their looks. You know that. Besides, the government limits how many Filipinos can emigrate, so there aren't many Filipino women here."

⚖ ⚖ ⚖

After taking care of Maria, I felt kind of down. It wasn't just about the bar-babe. I had this nagging feeling there would be more arrests. I wondered where it would all end. Who would be next?

Chapter Four

When I walked through the main entrance of Garfield on Monday morning, my mind was still churning about babysitting for the Caceres family. Little Maria and her father were okay, but more members of the Cannery Workers Union had been arrested. I wondered if members in Uncle Victor's union might get arrested too.

A picture of the woman with the stringy hair popped into my head. I didn't care what Mom said, I still didn't like her. I thought Anthony Avilá should have better taste. Even the flower she wore in her hair was ugly.

I was so wrapped up in all the things that had happened over the weekend, I wasn't paying attention when I passed Miss Libby's office. Miss Libby was the terror of Garfield. The mention of her name or glimpse of her shadow sent shivers up the spine of every student. She looked like a grandmother, not the sweet loving kind, but the mean kind. She was the truant officer for the school. Miss Libby had a huge bosom that made her look top-heavy and a voice you could hear bellowing through the hallways of the school. She had a cane for walking which she also used to snag her targets. That morning, because I was thinking about other things, she got me. Out came the cane and caught me by the arm, dragging me into her office.

"Miss Thompson, you're on the list."

"On my way to see you," I managed to croak.

She stared at me.

"I was. Really."

"You're supposed to check in if you're late."

She was talking about the day I helped clean up the union hall after the break-in. I got to school in time to take my test, but I had missed a couple of classes that morning, home room and library, but didn't think that was important. Still, we had to check in with the attendance office.

"I got to school late," I told her, "but in time to take my test."

"I thought you might be out on another holiday."

Because many kids from different cultures went to Garfield, the school gave excused absences for more holidays than the usual Christian ones. It turned out to be a gold mine. I found out when the Jewish and Oriental kids had holidays and asked to be excused on those days and even on some of the Canadian holidays. This was easily accomplished by inventing a huge family of many religions, cultures and countries.

"No, no holiday. None that I can think of."

She grimaced.

"Miss Thompson, look at this."

She produced an envelope. "These are your absence slips."

"Gee whiz, Miss Libby. I didn't know I'd been out that much."

"You're a smart girl, Josie. You could go far if you tried."

A few days earlier she had caught my friend Jennie Boggs and told her, "You're a good girl. You could make God proud if you tried." Jennie was a Negro, and Miss Libby had a different line for every nationality and race.

Miss Libby let me go after I promised to try harder. I had some business to take care of; I remembered a note from Principal Patterson's office telling me I had an appointment with him that morning.

Libby's office was just across the hall from the principal's office and I was hoping she didn't see me going in. As luck would have it, she had already caught another victim with her cane and was busily interrogating him.

Principal Patterson always looked like he had just stepped out of a shower. The wisps of his hair were combed perfectly over his bald spot, his shirt was starched, his pants had a sharp crease and he smelled like Lifebuoy soap.

He peered at me over gold-rimmed spectacles that sparkled in the light. "It seems you've been absent a lot, Miss Thompson." Watery blue eyes stared at me.

"I got a flu bug when we moved into town," I explained.

He thumbed through some papers. "That explains some of your absences, but not all of them."

The truth was, I had picked up another bug besides the influenza kind. I'd learned how to do the Bop and was infatuated with boys. As far as I knew, there were no inoculations for that kind of contagion, not that I wanted to be cured.

I told him what I told Miss Libby, "I'll try harder." I did want to do better, I just wasn't sure if I could. It was a lot of fun going to the Trianon and the New Orleans Club, listening to Lionel Hampton and Charles Brown, dancing until two in the morning. The problem was getting up the next day to get to school on time, or even keep interested in classes after meeting some swell guy. Boy, if Mom knew what I had been up to, I really would be in trouble. Several times when I stayed at Jennie's house we went out, and her mom never said anything. Although I knew it was wrong, I couldn't help myself. Jennie was lots of fun and very pretty. She attracted lots of boys. It was the first time I felt popular at school.

"Miss Thompson, you're a smart young lady. You test well in history and science." Principal Patterson peered over the gold spectacles. "But..." he fidgeted with papers, looking for his words, "I worry some of the other students may have too much influence on you."

His words were starting to sound a little different from the usual, "if you apply yourself you could do well," speech. He put the papers aside and removed his glasses while his eyes narrowed and glared.

He made me nervous. Mom had told me she imagined people in their underwear when they made her nervous. I closed my eyes for a second and I saw Principal Patterson in his boxer shorts, bony arms and legs sticking out from his underclothes. His boxers had little red hearts on them.

I smiled at him. "Sorry, I didn't catch what you said."

"I was talking about your friend, Miss Boggs, and some of the boys she knows. You would do well to stick to your own kind."

I knew who he was talking about. One boy in particular, a Negro kid named Bernard. The week before, during class change, I noticed the principal watching us. One wall of his office was almost entirely windows, which gave him a view of the main hallway. If you weren't changing classes or at lunch, he ripped out of his office demanding to know where you were going and why you weren't in class.

That day, Bernard and I were talking during lunch when he glared at us. Bernard was very dark. You could almost call his skin black, blue-black, and he had a Caribbean accent. We were talking and laughing about a singer, Roscoe Gordon, and his song *I Got Loaded*. At a show at the Eagle's Hall, the night before, Gordon appeared on stage in a rust-colored suit and was staggering like he was loaded or drunk or something. I guessed Bernard and I were having too much fun re-hashing the dance because Principal Patterson stared at us for the longest time.

"What's with him?" I asked Bernard.

"Let's get lost," he said.

⚖ ⚖ ⚖

When Principal Patterson told me that "I would do well to stick to my own kind," I knew right away what he was suggesting. He was talking about my friends Jennie Boggs and Bernard and some of the kids we hung out with in a mixed crowd.

"Exactly who are my own kind?" I finally said.

I guess he didn't expect me to speak up because he looked startled. He stood up and tried to stare me down. I got up, picked up my textbooks and stared back at him. "I don't have to listen to this." Then I started out of the office.

"I'm not done with you, young lady!"

I let the door shut hard as I left. The woman at the front desk stared at me. I nodded at her and made a bee-line to find Jennie. The old goat had made my stomach hurt. The things he said made it sound like some kids weren't as good as others. Garfield had so many neat kids going there. Why did someone like him ruin it?

It wasn't the first time Principal Patterson had shown his true self. There was a story that the year before he had called one of the football players, the star of the team, a n----r. The player knocked him out cold. Too bad, because he got kicked out of school and Garfield didn't even get into the play-offs.

⚖ ⚖ ⚖

I spotted Jennie walking down the hall. You couldn't miss her, even in a crowd. Her golden copper hair stood out like a fluorescent sign. A lot of kids thought she dyed her hair, but it was real. Her mom was white and her dad Negro. Her brother had that bright red hair, too.

"What happened? I saw you and the old goat, Patterson. It looked like you were arguing."

"The old goat was just babbling a lot of bull. Let's get out of here."

We took off for the Bulldog across the street from the school, to get a snack and talk over what happened with the principal. When we got there the place was jammed, so we sat on the lawn in back of the school. The band was suited up, practicing in the street. They not only sounded great, but they looked great in their deep purple uniforms. Garfield had won the nationals in band competition several years in a row. Bernard was tooting away on the trumpet. He couldn't wave but signaled by wiggling the instrument a little.

After the band passed, I told Jennie about my conversation with Principal Patterson. I told her everything, except what he said about her. No point in hurting her feelings.

"I got an idea," I said.

⚖️ ⚖️ ⚖️

The next day during lunch period a half dozen couples met in front of the principal's office. We paired up so we would be interracial couples, parading hand-in-hand and arm-in-arm, up and down the hall. Miss Libby came out of her office and stared at us. She held tight to her cane and looked like she wanted to smack someone. Principal Patterson glared at us for a while, then left his office and disappeared.

We paraded in front of the office for a couple of days. There wasn't anything the old duffer could do about it. After all, we were just walking and having fun like teenagers do.

Several kids joined us that were from the snooty Broadmoor neighborhood. They were students I really didn't like but I was glad they joined us. Maybe Mom was right, you can't really tell what a person is like by their looks or where they come from. There are other things that are more important.

⚖️ ⚖️ ⚖️

Goldie stopped by the house the day after our little demonstration.

"My son told me about your protest in front of Principal Patterson's office." He reached out and shook my hand. "Good going!"

"Thanks Goldie."

"My ex says a lot of parents are unhappy with the principal. They'd like to get him replaced."

"No kidding?"

"Ever since he insulted the football star and expelled him, and he's done other things."

Goldie's son Rocky, joined our little demonstration at school. We weren't friends, not even close, so I was surprised when he showed up and brought some other kids with him. He didn't like my mom going out with his dad, and I didn't like his dad going out with my mom. When we met in the hallways at school we nodded, but cut our eyes, just to make sure the other one knew we'd never be friends.

Sometimes Goldie picked Mom up and took her to work in the wee hours of the morning. Still dark out, he would drop her off a half a block away to make sure her boss, old man Goody, didn't see them together. Sometimes when he picked her up he parked around the corner by an empty warehouse; they had to sneak around to see each other. There weren't many places a Negro and white couple could go in public without getting harassed.

You wouldn't believe in this day and age some people were so backward. Even so, I don't know why they bothered. Goldie was a good person, but he was never going to take my Dad's place.

Chapter Five

It was Saturday night. Jennie and I had seen all the good movies and we hadn't heard about any parties. We decided to take the bus to town and go window shopping. There was the possibility something exciting might happen.

We got off the bus and walked to First Avenue hoping shops in the Pike Place Market were open. A few doors down from the market men dressed in funny blue uniforms poured out of an old hotel. There were about thirty of them. They surrounded Jennie and me and took up part of the street. They looked like sailors but the uniforms weren't any we'd seen before. They wore white hats with a red pom-pom on top. They laughed and pushed each other speaking a different language. I thought it was French. They eyed us.

"You are whores?" one of them asked with an accent.

Who are these disgusting guys?

One young man with big ears made a meal of Jennie with his eyes and licked his lips. He leaned close, asking, "Voulez-vous coucher avec moi?"

26

"Get away!" I told him. But Jennie flirted, showing a smile with deep dimples. "Jennie, come on. Let's split." I grabbed her arm.

"He's kinda cute," she protested.

"I think he asked if you want to go to bed with him."

Jennie backed away from him. "Shee-it. He can frig himself."

"Sea-going bellhop." I told Big Ears, and gave him a look that should have exploded his insides and melted him into a little ball on the pavement.

Some of the young men whistled, laughed and said more things we couldn't understand. We pushed our way through the crowd and left them still milling around on the sidewalk and part of the street.

They made me a sick. Who did they think they were? Who gave them the right to treat us like that - asking if we were whores!

We dog-trotted fast, into Pike Place Market. They didn't follow us, but it felt good to run and breath in the cool air. It helped to get rid of that nasty feeling of meeting them.

It was almost seven o'clock and most of the truck gardeners had already hosed down their stalls and closed shop. The market was deserted.

"Who the heck were those guys?" Jennie asked. "They looked like clowns."

"French sailors, I think. Something on the news about the French Navy picking up some airplanes for NATO maneuvers. "

"Those hats were stupid," she said.

"They were stupid."

⚖ ⚖ ⚖

With nothing open in the market we started to Third Avenue to the Bon Marche'. It stayed open late on Saturdays. The evening air was warm and you could smell and almost taste Puget Sound in the air.

"Mademoiselle, wait a moment," said a voice behind us. I turned to find two French sailors.

"Are you following us? Get lost," I said.

"Not so fast, this one's really cute," Jennie said, eyeing him.

He looked like he stepped out of a movie magazine. The sailor removed his hat and smiled at Jennie showing the whitest teeth. He even gave a little bow.

"Pardon, mademoiselle," the other one said to me. "A restaurant. Do you know where one is? Many are closing."

27

"Everything closes-up early. Seattle is just a big town," I told him. "You heard about rolling the sidewalks up at night?"

He nodded no, and stared blankly at me with a pair of the warmest brown eyes I had ever seen. His nose was broken, but he was handsome in a rugged sort of way.

Maybe there really is love at first sight....

"Miss, a restaurant - where?"

Nice voice....Eyes, brown....

"Miss?"

"Huh?"

"A place we might eat? Do you know?"

"There's a burger joint on Third Avenue."

"Alain," he said sticking out his hand. "And Jacques." His friend took Jennies hand in both of his. They laughed.

"Why aren't you with the rest of your buddies? Looking for whores?"

"Ladies of the evening?" He shook his head. "No. No."

I bet. "Nasty bunch, your friends."

"First time away from home. Most eighteen or nineteen years young."

"Still...."

"Yes. You are correct. In a foreign country is no excuse."

"You speak pretty good English."

"I went to school here and Canada."

"Look, we gotta go," I told him. It didn't look good standing on the street talking to sailors, even ones from France. People might think I was one of those ladies of the night....

"Come on, Jennie. We gotta go."

"First, a restaurant please." Alain said.

"Well, you go two blocks up, two over and there's a little place between Zales Diamond Store and the movie theater; it's kind of hard to find. Forget it, follow us. We're going that way, anyway."

As we walked to Third Avenue, Alain asked about school and what I was studying. I told him, "Lies mostly." He laughed the biggest laugh.

"Sounds like when I went to school here. There was a general strike in Seattle - yes?"

I nodded.

"Did they teach you about it in school?"

"I learned from my uncle," I answered.

"Me too, from my dad."

"Where you're from - France. What was it like during the war?"

28

"Mother and I lived in Canada until it was over. After the war we moved to Paris. Un oncle, une tante-uhh,my aunt and uncle, very old. We went to help."

"What was it like then, so soon after the war?"

"I was a student. Many buildings were gone, broken. Many strikes and riots. One May Day - you have May Day here?"

"Yes."

"May Day we students march. Thousands. I go with the red flag, the communiste - we fight for housing, food, jobs, rebuild schools."

"We had big May Day march in Seattle right after the war. I was a little kid. I think they asked for the same things. Big housing shortage. No jobs."

When we got to the burger joint Alain and Jacques invited us to eat with them. They seemed like nice guys even if they were in the navy, so we agreed.

The booths were small. The four of us squeezed into one but there was hardly enough room to move your elbows.

The place was long and narrow, with booths on one side and a counter running the length of the room. The kitchen was in the rear. Our waitress had wrinkles and crow's feet around her eyes. Her hair was plastered to her wet forehead. She was the only server and the place was packed.

"Okay kids, what can I getcha?" She whipped out an ordering pad from her pocket and pulled a pencil stuck behind her ear.

The guys ordered hamburgers and fries. Alain told Jacques they were traditional. Jennie wanted a hot dog and I wanted eggs and bacon.

Our waitress yelled to the cook in the rear, "Cookie! Two hockey pucks. Do you want onions with that?" she asked the boys. They nodded yes. "Make it cry, Cookie. And one bow-wow and a cluck and grunt!" She gave us each a glass of water with ice and hurried to the next customer.

Jacques' English was about as intelligible as the waitress's orders. Jennie did most of the talking while Jacques made faces at her. They did a lot of giggling until they were almost hysterical. Alain and I could hardly hear over their laughter and when a booth next to us was empty, we moved.

"So, why is the French Navy in Seattle?" I asked.

"Something to do with NATO," he said.

"It was on the news. My family is very political. We always listen to the news and talk about things going on in the world."

"Yes," Alain said. "Mother thinks more wars are coming."

"Doesn't that bother you?"

"I dreamed about the sea. Sailing on big ships."

"When your ship leaves, where will you go?"

"Maybe Algeria, maybe French-Indo China, maybe home. Wherever the Imperialists need us - that's where we go."

"Doesn't it bother you? Going to war for fat cats?"

"I didn't think wars would come so soon. Mother is mad at me for joining."

⚖️ ⚖️ ⚖️

Jennie wasn't one to sit quietly and evidently Jacques wasn't either. They finished their food and decided to go window shopping. Alain and I stayed in the café, ordering coffee, then dessert, then more coffee, and more dessert. At 10:00 p.m. the waitress told us they were closing.

We went to the bus stop at Third and Pike Street where we had agreed to meet Jennie and Jacques. We talked about so many things I felt like Alain was an old friend. His dad had gone to Spain like my dad. After the war in Spain was lost, his dad enlisted in the U.S. Army and was killed. When he told me this, I felt tears welling up. He looked away and was quiet.

When Jennie and Jacques arrived, we four stood and talked until time for the last bus home. I didn't want this meeting to end. "Why don't you and Jacques come for dinner tomorrow? My mom and aunt are great cooks!"

"They won't mind?" Alain asked.

"They'll love meeting the two of you."

We always had company at our house. People often dropped in unexpectedly. There was food for everyone, no matter how many. I don't know how Aunt C and mom did it, but they did.

We waved goodbye and got the bus home. I didn't want to go, but when Alain and Jacques promised to visit the next day I felt better. I was sure my family would want to meet my new friend. During our talk over coffee and dessert I learned he and his mother knew some of the union leaders in Vancouver that Uncle Victor knew.

⚖️ ⚖️ ⚖️

The next day I kept glancing at the clock.

"Don't worry," Aunt C said, "he probably had trouble finding the address. You don't always give the best directions."

Alain was a half hour late. While I was sitting on the front porch I saw a figure coming down the sidewalk. It took me a minute to recognize him because he was no longer wearing the clown naval uniform. I was relieved to see him in civvies; it doesn't do a girl's reputation any good to be seen with a serviceman, from any country.

"Alain!" I waved and ran to meet him.

"Sorry I'm late. I got lost."

"Where's Jacques?"

"He went to Jennie's house. They will come later."

He carried a package wrapped in brown paper. "What is that?"

"Wine. Mother says never go with your hand empty for dinner."

"Aunt C's gonna like you." She was setting the dining table in the front room. Alain called her mademoiselle after I introduced him and she gave him the biggest smile.

"What's this?" She asked when he handed her the bottle wrapped in paper.

"Wine from Burgundy."

"Where on earth did you get it? You can't buy any kind of alcohol in Seattle on Sunday. You can't buy wine like this anytime!" She rolled the bottle over, examining the label.

"I know important people," Alain told her. "I am friends with the ship's cook."

⚖️ ⚖️ ⚖️

Jennie and Jacques arrived just as dinner was on the table. After introductions were made all around, Aunt C poured glasses of wine for everyone, except Jennie and me. She made a toast to our two special guests from France.

After dinner Alain and Uncle Victor started talking about the war. Jacques and Jennie looked bored and excused themselves to go for a walk. As soon as Uncle Victor found out Alain's father was in the Lincoln Brigade in Spain and fought in the Second World War he started asking him a lot of questions. I realized I couldn't pry the two of them apart, so I went to the kitchen to help mom and Aunt C clean up.

"What do you think of him?" I asked.

"Really nice," Aunt C said, "and smart, too."

"Nice, but kind of old for you," Mom said.

31

"He's twenty. Not that much older," I answered.

"A lot of difference between fifteen and twenty," Mom cautioned.

Aunt C said, "She isn't going to do anything stupid."

⚖️ ⚖️ ⚖️

When I realized Uncle Victor and Alain were never going to quit talking, I marched into the living room and took Alain by the arm. "My turn," I told Uncle Victor, leading my friend to the porch.

"Thanks," Alain said. "I like your uncle a lot, but I came to see you."

"Sure it wasn't for the home-cooked meal?"

"Your aunt, Celeste - very good cook - ála Bonne Femme."

"What does that mean?"

"A cooking term. Food done by housewives."

"Is that good or bad?"

"Most fancy foods came from home cooks first," he explained.

"How did you know that? Does everybody in France know about food?"

He chuckled. "Mother runs a restaurant for her uncle and aunt. She wanted me to be a chef. I didn't want to cook. I joined the Navy."

⚖️ ⚖️ ⚖️

We sat on the steps until the stars came out. He told me how the constellations were different in other parts of the world and how it was odd seeing the Southern Cross instead of the North Star and the Big Dipper. We talked until it was time for the last bus back to town.

"Your ship leaves tomorrow?" I asked, knowing full well it did.

He nodded. "I think it's time to go," he said, checking his wrist watch. "I told Jacques we'd meet in town."

When he said goodbye to the family I could tell they liked him, because Mom and Aunt C hugged him. Uncle Victor shook his hand and clapped him on the back. "Take care of yourself," he told him.

"You as well," Alain replied. "Good luck with the government hearings you mention."

The bus stop was a half block away from the house. We stood near a Japanese Maple growing in the parking strip. A street lamp made shadows through the leaves like lace. Alain put his arms around me and held me close. I could feel his heart beating. We kissed. I didn't want to stop, I wanted it to last forever. Alain pulled away and kissed my hair.

"The bus is coming." He pointed to two headlights and a lit-up bus making its way down the hill toward us.

"You'll write? Promise!"

"I promise," he said. He gave me a quick goodbye kiss and stepped up into the bus.

I watched the vehicle climb the hill and disappear. Clouds covered the moon as I walked slowly down the dark sidewalk to the house. I could still feel the warmth of his mouth on mine.

Chapter Six

Mom and I huddled together in the back seat of the Willys with a blanket over us. There was a chill in the air, and the car heater didn't work. I was happy Mom had time off to go with me to the Paul Robeson concert.

It was too dark to see Mount Rainier. The only thing on the skyline was the big red R on the top of the Rainier Brewery.

Part of the trip to Peace Arch Park was on the new interstate highway. Only a section of it was finished. When we got to the entrance of the freeway, Uncle Victor sped up so we could merge at the same speed as the cars already traveling the highway. A lot of drivers weren't used to the new way of driving and slowed down; some even stopped instead of merging.

We crossed the bridge over the canal into the University District. A million pinpoints of lights shone on the lake. The stores were closed, but a neon sign over the Blue Moon Tavern showed an almost naked lady sitting on a crescent moon.

The Willys putted along while other cars zipped by us. The interstate ended a little past Everett and we found ourselves back on Highway 99 driving through fields of tulips. A giant billboard proclaimed it Tulip Capital of the World.

"Hey, there's one," Mom said, pointing to some Burma Shave signs. Each sign had a saying on it. The signs were spaced 30 or 40 feet apart, usually a half-dozen of them. Mom read this one out loud: "My job/ is keeping/ faces clean/ and nobody knows/ de stubble/ I've seen/ Burma Shave!"

Everybody laughed. It was nice to see her having fun; she worked so hard.

Aunt C and Uncle Victor were hugging, sitting close, his arm around her. They were whispering and giggling like a couple of teenagers. They were always doing that. I wondered if Alain and I would do that if we got married.

When we got to Bellingham, we drove to Western Washington College where my friend Red was going to school. He was only a couple of years older than me, but he had skipped and was already a freshman in college.

His real name was Henry Wolfe, but everybody called him Red because of the mop of red-orange hair. We had been friends forever, ever since I was six and he was eight, and we chased each other through the woods at a picnic. He had hit me in the back with a dead bird. It was love at first sight - his, not mine. He was my best and oldest friend.

We found his address on Garden Street, and there he was outside waiting for us. He climbed into the back with Mom and me. It was a tight fit; he was tall and skinny but his shoulders were broad. Bits of unruly red hair stuck out from under his Rainiers baseball hat.

"What's up cuz?" I nudged him in the ribs. I had known him so long it felt like we were related.

"You think everything will be okay at the concert?" he asked.

"That's why we're early," Uncle Victor told him, "To make sure it's okay. There will be a lot of fellas from the union too.

"Josie," Red said pointing, "that's Seholm Hill. I heard the Klan burned crosses up there in the old days."

"The Klan? In Bellingham? This isn't the South!"

"They went after the Wobblies and the Catholics. That was years ago," Mom said.

"Don't worry," Uncle Victor said. "If anyone like that tries anything, the hard rock miners from Canada will take care of it. They aren't going to let anyone start trouble for Robeson."

I got a chill. A lot of people were hurt when goons attacked Robeson's concert at Peekskill. Afterward, Robeson said, "I'm going to sing wherever people want me to sing - and I won't be frightened by crosses burning in Peekskill or anywhere else."

⚖ ⚖ ⚖

There was hardly anyone in the park when we arrived so Red and I decided to explore. He leaned against the boundary marker between the U.S. and Canada. I jumped back and forth across the line, from one country to another. We took pictures of ourselves standing with one foot in each country. When we got enough pictures we went for a walk. It was still a few hours until the concert was due to start.

Red and I hadn't seen each other for a few weeks. He had been trying to grow a mustache for the longest time and when I looked real close there was something above his upper lip.

"Hey, what's that above your lip?"

"What?"

"Is that eyebrow pencil?"

"Certainly not!"

I almost fell on the ground laughing.

After I quit laughing about eyebrow penciling his mustache, I told him about Jennie and me meeting the French sailors.

"You'll like Alain," I said, "He's political, like us."

Red looked upset and there was a long silence before we spoke again. He kept looking at the ground and kicking dirt. I knew how he felt about me, and I loved him too, but only like a brother.

"My grades are gonna be crap," I told him, changing the subject.

"What's going on, Joz? You usually do well in school."

"It doesn't seem important, with everything going on. Uncle Victor might go to jail."

"That's not for sure."

"I can't concentrate. It isn't just school…."

I told him how my ace, Jennie, and I had snuck in to see Charles Brown and Lionel Hampton at the Trianon Ballroom and then we couldn't get up in time for school. Jennie and I weren't the only ones who snuck in; half the kids from school were there. Booze wasn't sold at the ballroom, so ID's weren't checked very closely, if at all.

I confessed I thought about not coming to the concert, I wanted to hang out with Jennie. But I didn't tell him it was because I wanted to learn some new dance steps.

"You're lucky to be here," he said. "I got a letter from my brother in Korea; he said he'd give his seat in Hell to hear Robeson sing."

"Don't be ticked at me, Red."

"I'm not ticked." His voice got low and he started kicking dirt again, "I never get ticked at you."

We walked through a rose garden in the park, then down to the bay, and tried to skip stones on the water.

"Did I tell you I babysat for Mr. Caceres' little girl, Maria, while he was in jail?"

"Did you meet him?"

"No, but he called me the next day, to thank me."

"Neat."

"What's happening with your mom? Are they still trying to deport her?"

"After Britain refused to take her, the immigration has been trying to send her to Canada."

"Can they do that?"

"Like everything else, it's not kosher, but they do it anyway. Like they did with Robeson, not allowing him to travel outside the U.S. and the cannery workers - the government brought them here, they aren't immigrants - now they want to get rid of them after they demanded their rights."

⚖ ⚖ ⚖

When we got back to the Peace Arch, the park was filled with people, and Uncle Victor was on the stage at the microphone. He said Robeson would arrive soon. He pointed toward the Canadian side of the park where there were several hundred men, dressed in work clothes and wearing miner's hats carrying hammers in their hands. "The Canadian Miners Union is here to welcome Robeson," he said.

They marched toward us, singing:

Arise ye prisoners of starvation,
Arise ye wretched of the earth,
For justice thunders condemnation...

You heard that song on May Day and at big events, especially when people from other countries were present.

Someone in the crowd cried out, "There's Robeson." Everybody turned to see the big man, with a wide smile, walking toward us. Men from Uncle Victor's and Goldie's union escorted him; it looked like the United Nations. There were Negroes, whites and Oriental guys. Even with all those people around him, it was easy to spot Robeson because he was at least a foot taller than everybody else.

As they made their way to the stage, the crowd parted like in the story about the Red Sea. Everybody jumped to their feet, cheering. The air seemed to crackle. It was thrilling seeing someone so famous up close.

Robeson was one of the greatest singers and actors in the world, and he had friends like Einstein, but still hung out with ordinary people too. When he came to Seattle, he didn't stay in fancy hotels. In fact, he stayed at Goldie's house. I'd sat in the same chair Robeson sat in when he visited and heard about the stories he told. Robeson was very outspoken. He spoke out about racism and injustice everywhere he went, and that was all around the world.

Before Robeson sang, Goldie introduced a man from the Canadian Miners Union who thanked the union members from both sides of the line for coming to the concert and supporting Robeson's right to travel.

When Robeson began his first song, he cupped his hand behind his right ear.

"Why is he doing that?" I asked Mom.

"So he can hear his own voice and make sure he's on key," she explained.

I'd heard him on his records, but never in person. He began the concert with a lullaby. His voice was so soft you could see a little baby sleeping, and feel the cradle rocking in the breeze.

He knew a dozen languages, and sang to us in Spanish, German, Yiddish, Russian, Welsh and Chinese - songs from all over the world.

Alain said he had heard him sing with the Welsh miners in Wales.

"This song doesn't need any introduction," Robeson said. He sang:
I dreamed I saw Joe Hill last night,
Alive as you and me.
Says I, "But Joe, you're ten years dead."
"I never died," said he,

"I never died," said he.

Uncle Victor told me he heard people all over the world singing Joe Hill. Everybody knew about the I.W.W. organizer killed by the copper bosses in Utah. The crowd sang with him. It felt like being in church. A man dressed in bib overalls sitting next to me wiped his eyes. I elbowed Aunt C to look at him.

"I know him," she said, "big Yugoslav family, coal miners. His dad was shot organizing the union."

He wasn't the only man I saw wipe away tears.

Robeson sang *The Peat Bog Soldiers.*

Far and wide as the eye can wander,
Heath and bog are everywhere.
Not a bird sings out to cheer us.
Oaks are standing gaunt and bare.

It's the only song ever composed in a concentration camp.

Robeson said German volunteers in the International Brigades brought the song to Spain and it became the Republican anthem. Uncle Victor had told me Robeson went to Spain during the war. It was on a Christmas Day and the war stopped for two hours while he gave a concert; both sides put down their arms and listened. I thought of my dad and wondered if he had heard Robeson on that Christmas Day in Spain.

He ended the concert with the death scene from Shakespeare's Othello. He said it was a soliloquy. Red and I edged our way a little closer. Here was one of the most famous people in the whole world, and we were only a few feet from him! Robeson bent his head, until the crowd was quiet. There were 20 or 30 thousand people, and it was so quiet all you could hear were the waves lapping in the bay and the far-away cry of a seagull. Robeson's voice made you feel like you were hypnotized. I saw him wearing a crown, and dressed like a king. He was in a room with beautiful curtains. There was a sword in his hands.

"One that loved not wisely but too well." Words floated like a dream. Then he sounded angry, "I took by the throat the ...dog, and smote him, thus!"

He stabbed himself with the sword. Swear to God, cross my heart and hope to die, he killed himself.

"No!" I yelled.

Everyone was standing, cheering and applauding. I couldn't believe it, but for an instant, I truly thought he had killed himself.

"You okay?" Red asked.

People crowded around Robeson after the concert. Uncle Victor was standing next to him, so I grabbed Red's arm and we jumped up on the stage. He was even taller than I thought and his voice was warm and friendly. I swallowed and got up my courage.

"Mr. Robeson, how did you do that, make that death scene seem real?"

He chuckled. "Lots of practice - and sometimes a bit of luck."

Uncle Victor introduced us, "Paul, this is my niece, Josie, and her friend, Red." Robeson shook our hands.

"Are you students?" he asked. Red told him he was in college and I told him about high school. "It's hard to study, when so much is happening in the world," I blurted out.

"Learning is important," he said.

"What about the lies? Especially history?" I asked.

"Then look for the truth, don't let anyone stop you," he flashed a big smile. "Nice meeting you both." He shook hands again. More people climbed up to meet him so we left.

"I can't believe it, Red. We talked to Robeson; he shook our hands and gave us advice."

Red had a big grin too.

"I'm not going to wash my hand for a month." I told him, "This is the hand that shook the hand of Paul Robeson!"

"You're a nut!" Red said, still grinning.

⚖ ⚖ ⚖

After the concert was over, Aunt C, Mom and I visited with friends we hadn't seen for a long time. Uncle Victor called Red, and the two of them disappeared. The crowd was thinning down by the time we got in the Willys and we met up with Uncle Victor and Red. I asked Uncle Victor if everything was safe. This was exactly the way it happened in Peekskill: people were attacked as they were leaving. Goons from the American Legion and VFW and the Klan bashed them with rocks, bats and bricks.

"Don't worry, it's fine," Uncle Victor said. "Red will tell you. We scouted around just before we got ready to leave."

Red said, "I asked some folks in Blaine if they thought the VFW or the Legion was going to attack Robeson. They told me, Are you kidding? Did you see all those miners protecting him? And the hammers?"

⚖ ⚖ ⚖

Red was unusually quiet on the ride into Bellingham, "Are you okay?" I asked.

"Got a headache. Anyone got an aspirin?"

I was sorry about his headache, but it was going to set Uncle Victor off on a lecture. Normally he doesn't lecture people, but he felt strongly about letting nature take its course. He said taking pills would interfere with the body healing itself.

"Have you tried deep breathing?" Uncle Victor asked. "When you get home, put a cold washcloth on your forehead. Try relaxing and breathing from deep down, in your stomach. It takes a while, but it works. It's best to stay away from chemicals if you can."

I poked Red, handing him a couple of aspirin I had because of a toothache. He swallowed them down dry when Uncle Victor wasn't looking.

We let Red out, and he said he'd see me next weekend.

⚖ ⚖ ⚖

It was night by the time we got back to the city. It had been a long day, but I was wide awake. The city lights were brighter than usual, and the salt air seemed fresher. Everything seemed like it was new. Alain's face popped into my head.

Chapter Seven

"Josie," Aunt C called from the kitchen, "If you want a snack, bread's right out of the oven."

I could have eaten a whole loaf of homemade bread by myself, especially when it was right out of the oven and slathered with butter. I threw my school books on the telephone table and noticed an envelope peeking out from the stack of mail. On the upper left-hand corner a few words stood out: lettre and R. Fournier. The envelope was small and lightweight; it felt like a feather in my hand.

"Josie, are you hungry?" Aunt C called.

"Back in a sec." Ordinarily it would have taken an army to keep me from freshly baked bread; instead I took the stairs, two at a time, my heart racing. The return address was R. Fournier. It was from Alain!

I threw myself on the bed holding the letter tight, against my heart. I smelled it. I made a wish, make it say good things, make it say "I miss you," make it say "I love you"

I was afraid to open it. There was a stamp with a picture of the Eiffel Tower and some writing I couldn't understand.

I found a pair of sharp scissors, inserted one of the blades carefully into the top of the envelope, and slit it open. There were three pages written on paper as thin as tracing paper. I unfolded the letter to find neat, almost fancy handwriting.

Dear Josette:

We were at sea for a long time. I'm sorry it took so long for you to hear from me. One of our destinations was French-Indochina which the locals call Viet Nam. The Vietnamese food was interesting and good. Of course there was plenty of French food, as this beautiful country has been a colony of France for a long time. The northern part is run by a man named Ho Chi Minh; he was elected the president after the war ended. He is not well known outside his country but the locals agree he will succeed in liberating them. It seems they have been at war for independence for over 50 years. Despite the fighting, the country is beautiful. So are the people. While we were docked I saw Vietnamese men unloading sacks of coal on their backs. All the while there was a winch on the ship and a crane on the dock nearby. I guess it was cheaper to use human labor than run the machines. I arrived home yesterday. My thoughts have been of you and your family. Please give my regards to your mother and aunt and tell Victor I have a lot to tell him when we meet again. Our time together was too short. I see your face in my mind, but it would be nice if you could send a photograph and I will do the same. There was a picture you showed me in an album, of you in shorts. You have gorgeous legs, or as they say in the movies, gams! But any picture you send would be appreciated. I told my mother about you and your family. Tomorrow she is going to see if she can find a scarf for you which I will send under separate cover. We are known for beautiful silk scarves, although they are hard to find since the war.

With love, Alain

I looked at the words "With love" and read it over and over until Aunt C shouted, "Josie, did you hear me? There's homemade bread!"

I carefully folded the letter, slipped it back into the envelope, and placed it under my pillow.

Chapter Eight

I woke up with the sun shining through the window. I felt like singing. Alain had written. I had read his letter to Aunt C, to Mom and to Uncle Victor. Then I re-read it a hundred times. Maybe it was a thousand. He signed the letter, "With love." I leaped out of bed, dressed quickly and headed downstairs.

Uncle Victor and Aunt C were at the yellow Formica table.

"Morning, great day!" I said.

Aunt C asked if I wanted to go to the Pike Place Market. I was planning on meeting Jennie and listening to a new Clovers' record. I felt like dancing and I wanted to tell her all about the letter. But Aunt C looked so worried that I agreed to go to the market. I knew it was about Uncle Victor. The hearings were starting in a few days. Then we would know if Uncle Victor was going to go to jail or not.

On the way to the bus we stopped at Pete's Corner Store. I liked Pete. He was one of those guys who talked a lot. He gave his opinion often, and loud.

Aunt C put a pack of Camels on the counter and started looking through her purse for money. Pete told Aunt C, "Two men were here. They showed badges, G-Men. They asked me to take down license numbers of people who visit you."

"The FBI. Did they threaten you?"

"I told them to get the hell out. I was paid to kill Fascists in the war. By God, I thought that would be the end of them!"

"I'm sorry, Pete."

"Put your money away." He stuffed the pack of cigarettes into her open purse. "Be careful, those are bad fellas."

⚖️　⚖️　⚖️

By the time we got downtown it was sprinkling. When we got to the Pike Place market it was pouring. The open air stalls were covered and the rain made a drumming sound on the tin roof.

Shoppers haggled over price. It was like a carnival, the men in the stalls trying to out-do one another. They shouted, insulted each other, made jokes and even sang; anything to attract buyers to their stall. Usually Aunt C and I had a good time kidding around with them, but not that day. When we got to the Seafood Grotto, two of the butchers were in the middle of their "world famous salmon toss." They threw a big salmon back and forth. One of the guys looked the fish in the face and said, "You look pretty fishy to me." He tossed the fish.

The other one caught it, and said, "What's the difference between a fish and a piano?"

"You can't tuna fish," his partner answered. The crowd hooted and laughed.

The place was packed with tourists. We had to elbow our way through the crowd before we finally we got to Mrs. Fujimoto's stall. She and Aunt C were friends before Mrs. Fujimoto and her family were sent to the relocation camps during the war. She told us a lot about the camps. She said the reason there were Victory Gardens during the war was that the Japanese truck farmers were all in the camps. That caused a vegetable shortage on the west coast. Some people moved onto the Fujimoto family's land, but they didn't know how to farm it, or they didn't want to do the back-breaking work.

Mrs. Fujimoto refused money for the vegetables Aunt C wanted. "Donation for Victor," she said. She leaned close and whispered something to Aunt C. Aunt C thanked her for the vegetables, but she looked upset.

When we got back to the Seafood Grotto, an even larger crowd waited for the fish toss. One of the cute fish butchers whistled at me and Aunt C. He always stopped us and we would joke with him. He winked and said, "Hubba, hubba."

"Drop dead!" Aunt C answered. There were tears in her eyes. The butcher looked crushed.

"I'm sorry," she told him. "I'm not myself today."

"Aunt C, what's wrong?" I felt worried.

"Sorry. We're never getting through this crowd," she said.

"Let's go to the Vesuvius," I suggested. "We can have lunch and maybe the crowds will thin out."

"I haven't eaten all day," she admitted.

The Vesuvius was our favorite restaurant. Aunt C said it was the best kept secret in Seattle. It served terrific Greek food, and it was inexpensive. A few tourists might wander in, but mostly locals ate at the old tables with mismatched china and silverware. It was almost noon, and the place was packed with businessmen in suits sitting near the bar. There were lots of drinks and beer bottles on the tables. They were laughing, talking loud, and telling dirty jokes. Occasionally, one of them made a racist remark.

"Idiots," Aunt C muttered. We made our way around the tables to a side room with small booths against a wall of floor-to-ceiling windows that overlooked Elliott Bay. The room was empty, so we had our pick of the booths.

No amount of rain or wind kept the ferries and sailboats on the bay below us from plowing across the Sound. The water and the sky were the same gray color; you couldn't tell where one began and the other ended. Raindrops made zigzag paths down the window-panes.

Our waiter arrived. He was tall and thin and had deep pock marks on his face. "What can I do ya for?" he asked. He knew us and didn't bother putting the menus on the table. "Let me guess, pot of tea, Moussaka and Beef Stifado?"

Aunt C nodded.

"Right away then, hon."

He brought hot tea while we waited for our food. After Aunt C drank some she looked like her old self.

"I've been having nightmares," she confided.

"About someone chasing you?"

"This time I'm on a boat and all the passengers are women. They're gray, their skin, their clothes. It's a ship going to the prison; they go to visit their husbands and sons. When the ship docks, everyone gets up at the same time, eyes ahead, not talking, like they're dead."

Our waiter arrived with the food.

"Dreams can seem real," I said.

"Sorry Josie. Let's enjoy our food."

After we ate, I remembered Mrs. Fujimoto whispering to Aunt C "What did Mrs. Fujimoto say to you?"

"I know she didn't mean to, but she made me feel worse. There's a bill in Congress, The Detention Camp Bill, to detain subversive elements. She's worried Victor might be put in a camp, like the Japanese."

⚖   ⚖   ⚖

When we left the Vesuvius, I suggested we take the lower level route out of the market. Aunt C had never gone that way.

I showed her the steps down to the lower level. Most of these stores sold second-hand clothes, books and comics. A lot of them were empty. It smelled musty, but it was warm and bright. I liked it because it was kind of secret; not many people went down to the lower level.

"And where did you say this goes?" Aunt C asked. "This place is a rabbit warren."

"It goes under the cobblestone street, Pike Place, then under more shops, and comes out where you'd never guess. It'll be a surprise," I told her.

We came upon an old man sitting propped up against the wall, an empty whiskey bottle next to him.

"Lady, I really need a drink," he said, sticking out his hand. Aunt C dropped a couple of coins into his shaking hand. He pulled himself up and wobbled away.

"Why'd you give him money for booze?"

"He's got the DTs." she said, "He'll be pretty sick without a drink. How much further?"

We rounded a corner where the exit door was just ahead. An old lady blocked our way. Her clothes were lumpy. She wore three or four dresses, one on top of the other; a long red scarf was draped around her neck. She held both arms up for us to stop.

"Excuse us," Aunt C said.

The old lady shoved a torn picture of Jesus into Aunt C's face. "Have you been saved?" she demanded.

"Please move," Aunt C said. "We're in a hurry."

"Get right with your maker," the old lady wailed.

Aunt C reached her arm around the woman and pulled open the door, pushing past her. She grabbed Aunt C by the coat. "Get right with God!" the woman cried. "Do it, before it's too late."

Aunt C glared.

The old lady let go of her coat and started babbling into her red scarf.

Once through the door, we were inside a cigar store on First Avenue. I thought Aunt C would get a kick out of exiting into a store, but the old lady had ruined my little surprise.

"What a loony," Aunt C said. "Promise me you won't go down there by yourself."

I had walked through the lower level of the market a zillion times and never ran into any crazy people like the old lady. But I promised, anyway.

We could still hear the old lady screeching on the other side of the closed door. "Get right with God! Before it's too late."

"Let's get the hell outta here," Aunt C said.

⚖ ⚖ ⚖

The rain had stopped, and everything smelled new and fresh. The sun was peeking through the clouds. There's a saying in Seattle: If you don't like the weather, wait five minutes.

We walked to Cherry Street to catch the bus home. We were almost home when it started pouring again. "Darn," Aunt C said. "These bags will melt in the rain. She checked the two shopping bags full of vegetables Mrs. Fujimoto had given us.

It was raining hard when we stepped out of the bus. Raindrops bounced a foot in the air when they landed. The street and gutters overflowed and water ran down the middle of the sidewalk. We ran, heads down, hoping to get inside before the shopping bags gave out. There was a bright bolt of lightning and a crack of thunder just as we reached the steps.

We were on the front porch when we saw the front door was wide open.

"What the hell?" she said.

There was a police car under the madrona tree and an ambulance in the driveway. Aunt C dropped the shopping bags on the living room floor. They ripped open and onions and potatoes rolled out across the floor. Mom, Goldie and some uniformed men were crowded around the spare room Uncle Victor used as an office.

Aunt C rushed to Mom. "Terry, what the hell?"

Mom threw her arms around Aunt C. "There's been an accident. Doctor Harmon is here, examining him now."

The door was open. I could see Uncle Victor on the floor, face down. Aunt C pulled out of Mom's arms and went to kneel beside Uncle Victor's still body. Doctor Harmon was bent over him, listening with a stethoscope. He removed the scope from his ears, and shook his head. "I'm sorry," he said.

⚖ ⚖ ⚖

We gathered in the living room to hear what Doctor Harmon had to say. Aunt C stopped sobbing, but her face was wet and her eyes were full of tears. Goldie sat next to her and Mom put her arms around me as the doctor talked. He had put on his raincoat and hat and stood in the center of the room holding his black bag. He looked at Aunt C when he spoke. "It appears your husband may have mistakenly taken an overdose of sleeping tablets. This sometimes...."

Mom interrupted, "That couldn't be."

"It doesn't happen often, but it's not unusual for someone groggy to take more pills than they realize."

"But Victor never took pills, of any kind," Mom insisted.

The doctor looked sad. "I'm very sorry. We'll know more when we get the medical examiner's report," he explained. He went to Aunt C and gave her a small bottle. "Something to help you cope." He patted her shoulder and started to the door.

"He never took pills," I screamed. "You're a liar!"

Slowly the door closed behind him.

Chapter Nine

When I was a baby, my dad died. I missed having a dad, but it wasn't the same as if I'd gotten to know him.

Great Grandma Abigail passed away when I was eight. I remember Great Grandma smelled like peppermint, the pink kind. When Great Grandma passed away, Mom looked so sad I made myself cry. It seemed like the right thing to do.

It's different with Uncle Victor. I can't stop crying, and I feel something I've never felt before. I feel like I'm wearing a suit of lead clothes, pressing on every nerve, every muscle and inch of skin. I'm not sure there is a name for how I feel, but it doesn't matter. All I know is, I want my Uncle Victor back.

⚖️ ⚖️ ⚖️

Things started to get a little better when Grandpa and Gramma came. They were Mom's and Aunt C's parents — my favorites. Actually, my only ones, as my dad's had passed away.

When they arrived it was late in the day, but I was still in my pajamas, sitting on the landing staring at the picture of Uncle Victor. I would never again feel his whiskers when he hugged me, or hear him laugh. The tears started when I heard a booming voice coming from the kitchen.

"Too many loose ends, something smells rotten, like hell." It was Grandpa. He always talked loud, like he was shouting across a valley to a mountaintop.

Grandpa, Gramma and Mom were sitting at the table drinking coffee. There was a platter of cinnamon rolls in the center of the table. I broke into tears when I saw my grandparents. They both put their arms around me and hugged me until I quit crying. Grandpa patted me. "It's okay to cry," Grandma said. There were tears in her eyes. I tried to choke back the tears. Even though I stuttered, and the tears wouldn't stop, I asked about the cinnamon rolls.

"Gramma, did you bake these?"

She reached out and smoothed my hair in place. "Sit down. I'll make some cocoa to go with them."

While she was busy heating the milk for the cocoa, Grandpa and Mom started talking about Uncle Victor.

"I'm tellin' ya," Grandpa said, "there's something fishy about this whole thing."

"I know, Pop," Mom said. "we'll get the autopsy report soon. Then we'll know the truth about Victor's death."

"Until then, be careful," he insisted.

"Pop," Mom said with a sigh, "you worry too much."

"You said the window where they found him was wide open, and rain from the storm was tracked around the floor. Right?"

"There could be lots of explanations," Mom reasoned. "It was a bad storm; the wind might have pushed the water around."

"There was something else," I volunteered. "The Feds."

"What about them?" Mom asked.

"They never showed up to watch the house that morning."

"What do you mean?" Grandpa prodded.

"They watched the house every day and followed Uncle Victor everywhere. They weren't in their usual spot when Aunt C and I went to the market."

"You never know what tricks those birds are up to," Mom added.

"The only other time they didn't show up was when we went to the Peace Arch for the Robeson concert. Then we saw them up there. They knew where we were going."

"She's got a point," Grandpa said. "Maybe they did know something the day he died. Seems mighty suspicious."

Mom scowled at him, "If you're trying to scare us, you're doing a good job."

"This isn't a game," Grandpa growled. He reached into his shirt pocket for a pack of cigarettes. "There are forces that want to kill the unions. They don't care if they destroy a man's reputation or his life."

"Okay. Okay. I know you're right," Mom agreed.

"I just want you safe." He pulled out a wooden match, scratched the top with his thumbnail; it exploded into flame and lit up the Camel cigarette.

"Smoke out on the porch, will you, dear?" Gramma reminded him. She stroked his shoulder.

"Okay, okay," he grumbled, but managed a smile as he pushed his chair away from the table. He took his coffee with him as he headed to the porch. "When you finish your cocoa," he said to me. "Come and sit with an old man."

⚖ ⚖ ⚖

I sipped the hot cocoa and nibbled cinnamon rolls as Gramma questioned me. How was I feeling? Had I heard from my friends at school? Was I sleeping? Eating? I told her I was sad and feeling bad, like I had the flu, but I knew it wasn't because I didn't have a fever.

She put her hand on my forehead. "No, no temperature. When you lose someone you love, your whole body gets sick. Not like a cold or the flu - worse."

When we finished talking, I realized I had eaten four cinnamon rolls. "I forgot how good these were."

"I didn't forget. I know how much you like them." She smiled. "I baked them special, for you."

⚖ ⚖ ⚖

The screen door to the porch squeaked when I opened it. Grandpa looked up and smiled. He looked so sad before he knew I was on the porch.

"Sit here," he said, patting the spot next to him.

"I'm really glad you're here, Grandpa."

"Don't know how long I can stay. My neighbor is doing the milking and there's a heifer 'bout ready to drop her calf. Your grandma will stay until I get back."

"Good," I said. "That will make Aunt C feel better."

"Your aunt's taking it pretty hard...."

He looked sad again.

We sat for a long time, not talking until Grandpa brought up the Feds. "Josie, honey, tell me again why you thought it was so strange the Feds weren't there the day Victor died."

"Grandpa, they spy on us every day: rain, shine, lightning or snowstorm. And they don't show up on the day the biggest thing happens?"

Grandpa didn't say anything. He took another Camel from the pack and lit up. When he finished the cigarette, he snubbed it out and said, "Why don't we keep our ideas about the Feds to ourselves? Your mother and grandma worry too much." He turned to me, "And don't you worry, either." He put an arm around my shoulders. "Lots of people are here to help. Me, your grandma and Goldie, and many others."

I was still worried, but it made me feel better knowing someone understood what was bothering me. Grandpa called himself "the old Bolshevik." He worked in the woods and helped organize the logging camps. If he didn't know the score, no one did. Grandpa said things "smelled rotten," and that's what I think, too.

Goldie and an old friend of the family, Archie McCloud, came to pay their respects and Mom invited them for dinner. McCloud had been Uncle Victor's oldest friend. They went to the same high school, joined the army at the same time, and even wrote to each other all during the war. We didn't see him very often, as he lived north of Seattle, at Sedro Woolley, where he worked in a sawmill. He always smelled like sawdust and sometimes you could even see it in his hair.

After we ate, Grandma and Mom cleaned up the kitchen and sent Aunt C to take a nap. She looked tired, and there were dark circles under her eyes. She slept a lot, or sat staring into space.

Grandpa, Goldie and McCloud went to the porch where they could smoke. I trailed after them because it was way more important than doing the dishes. I knew they would talk about Uncle Victor's death and I needed to know exactly what happened.

"What's the low-down on this Dr. Harmon character?" Grandpa asked Goldie. "What happened that day?"

"Me and some guys from the union were to meet with Victor here at the house. When he didn't answer our knock, I figured he was in the back and couldn't hear us. I called out, but there was no answer, so I went to the back door. It was open and I called out again. When he still didn't answer I looked in the back room he uses for an office and found him sprawled out on the floor, face down, his glasses half off his face. I felt his carotid artery. No sign. You get so you can tell after you've seen so many during the war."

Goldie quit talking and looked sadder than I have ever seen. "I came by to let you know that whatever Celeste needs, let me know; the union owes Victor. I don't know what we're going to do without him. There's death benefits for the members, too. I'll fill out the paperwork and bring them by for her to sign."

"It's tough, when you're so close," Grandpa said. Goldie looked like he might cry. "What happened next, after you found him?"

Goldie swallowed and his voice quavered as he told him the rest. "I talked to the guys in the front room. We decided they should go back to the union hall, partly to leave before the authorities showed up, and to be at the hall to answer questions from members and the press when the story got out."

"Why didn't you want the other union members to be around when the authorities showed?" Grandpa frowned.

"We didn't want the leadership of the union getting tied up in an inquiry, or God knows what else."

Grandpa nodded agreement. "Good thinking."

Goldie's voice quit shaking, but he still looked like the tears might start. "After that I called Terry," he continued. "She left the bakery right away and arrived about twenty minutes later. I suggested we call Dr. Harmon. He could notify the authorities; then we could get an honest explanation from him about Victor's death, one we might not get from the cops. Harmon has a reputation of treating a lot of progressives. It seemed like a good idea to have a doctor here when Josie and Celeste got back from the market."

"Did Harmon examine him?"

"He did. Then he called the cops and coroner."

"What did he say about his exam? Did he say what caused his death?"

"He said he wouldn't be able to give a definitive answer until the autopsy was done. He thought it could be a reaction to medication; it could be any number of things. He was pretty vague."

I started to say something, but Grandpa gave me a look and held up his hand telling me to be quiet.

"And the open window?" Grandpa continued.

I didn't really think about it until later," Goldie said. "Then I remembered it was cold in the room and wondered why the window was wide open. Also, there was water on the floor from the rainstorm, almost like someone making tracks."

"Why do you think the doctor told Celeste and Josie it was an overdose?" Grandpa asked. "Everybody knew Victor didn't take any kind of pills, not even vitamins. Did you or Terry tell Harmon that?"

"We didn't get a chance; the cops, the coroner, and Celeste and Josie all came about the same time."

"Well now, we need to find out why the doc said it was an overdose," McCloud said.

"Aunt C has an appointment to see Doctor Harmon tomorrow," I volunteered.

"I wish she wouldn't see him," Grandpa said. "I haven't ever met him, but I don't trust the guy."

"Aunt Celeste likes him; he's been her doctor for a year now," I said.

"Right now she's not thinking clearly." Grandpa said.

The talk turned to other things and Goldie excused himself, to help with the clean-up in the kitchen.

"One more thing," Grandpa said, stopping him. "Do you think it was foul play?"

"Let's talk - later," Goldie said, glancing at me.

"Well, is it possible?" Grandpa insisted.

"Any thing's possible. Probable?" Goldie shrugged.

"Maybe we need some heavyweights around the house," Grandpa suggested.

Goldie and McCloud nodded. They went inside to help Mom and Gramma finish cleaning-up.

⚖ ⚖ ⚖

Grandpa lit another cigarette.

"When did you start smoking tailor-mades? I asked.

"When you weren't around to help me roll 'em," he said, smiling.

Grandpa used to buy Velvet Tobacco and I'd put the cigarette papers in a cigarette rolling machine, fill the paper with loose tobacco, slide the mechanism back and forth and, presto: a rolled cigarette. I liked making the cigarettes and lining them up like little logs. Grandpa would carefully pick them up and store them in an air-tight tin.

"Grandpa, do we really need someone to guard the house? Is that what you meant by having heavyweights around?"

"I'm going to ask McCloud to stick around for a while. If he and Goldie are visible, that ought to do it until the memorial. After that things should calm down."

Grandpa fidgeted in the seat next to me. I thought he might be having pain from his hip. Mom said he had a bad case of arthritis. "Why don't you stretch out?" I suggested, moving to the chair across from him. He put one leg up to rest on the swing and took a deep drag on the Camel. It had gotten dark and we sat quietly looking at the stars. The only sounds were crickets and gnats buzzing in the air.

"You really miss him, don't you?" Grandpa said.

"I really do." I felt hot tears gush down my cheeks and I hoped he wouldn't notice them.

"I miss him too," he said.

Uncle Victor always wrote to Grandpa and, whenever Grandpa came down the hill from the farm to Bellingham, he called Uncle on the phone. I'm sure they talked about the union and organizing because they always talked about that stuff. They were also fishing nuts, and Uncle Victor would ask what kind of fish were biting: steelhead, humpies, or kings. Grandpa and Uncle Victor were close, more like father and son than in-laws. Or as Grandpa called it "outlaws."

"Did I ever tell you about seeing your uncle fight in the Golden Gloves?"

"I never heard that one," I lied. I knew all of Grandpa's stories by heart. I could almost repeat them, word-for-word.

"Well," he began, "it was even before he met your Aunt C...."

Chapter Ten

Grandpa got a phone call from one of his neighbors, letting him know the cow he was concerned about had birthed her calf. When Grandpa told him he was returning to see about the animal, I could hear him yelling to Grandpa over the phone, "Listen you old coot, stay and take care of your family. I'll handle it." It was hard to believe they were good friends the way the man yelled. In the end, Grandpa agreed to let him take care of the calf. I was relieved he was going to stay with us.

Mom and Grandpa argued about Aunt C keeping her appointment with Dr. Harmon. She told him Aunt C wasn't going to change her mind, and if he kept insisting all it did was upset her. Grandpa wanted to go with Aunt C to Dr. Harmon's office.

"I'll go," I volunteered. Grandpa agreed and Mom looked relieved.

I remembered Dr. Harmon saying Uncle Victor was dead, and my screaming he was a liar. How could he say Uncle Victor died of an overdose of sleeping pills? Uncle Victor never took pills, not any kind.

On the way to the bus stop with Aunt C, we passed the Corner Store and Pete came out when he saw us.

"I'm so sorry about Victor," he said. "Let me know if there's anything I can do. I mean anything."

Aunt C and Pete usually talked for a long time, but today she hardly spoke. I told Pete we were late for an appointment, and we hurried down the block to the bus stop.

Old gas buses ran on Yesler Way. They coughed and groaned up the hills, then screeched their brakes all the way down steep Yesler Hill. On Third Avenue we caught the electric trolley going uptown. The ride was quiet and smooth. We got off right in front of Harmon's office building.

We were the only people on the elevator. We whizzed up to the sixth floor. My stomach did a flip-flop. Ordinarily I liked the sensation, but I was nervous about meeting the doctor and it made me queasy.

Our steps echoed as we walked down the marble tiled hallway, especially Aunt C's high heels. They did a rat-a-tat-tat, like a drummer.

Dr. Harmon's door had a pane of frosted glass with his name in black, outlined by gold: Carl H. Harmon, M.D. & Surgeon. The waiting room was full of patients. Most of the patients were women and kids, except one old man, who sat in a corner smoking, and trying to stay out of the line of fire of two little boys throwing blocks. Their mother pleaded with them to quit, but they kept right on.

"Been waiting long?" I asked the mom.

"A while; it seems longer." She rolled her eyes at the boys. "Don't you just love Dr. Harmon?"

I didn't say anything.

"Dr. Harmon delivered both my kids," she said. "He's a wonderful man. My husband was out of work when I had my last boy." She leaned close and whispered, "He let us make small payments and only charged us half. He told my husband and me, *Let's get this baby delivered; then, we'll worry about the money.*"

"Billy, don't do that," she cried. The boy put an ashtray back on its stand. The mom sighed, leaping after the other one, who crawled to a low table and started stuffing paper into his mouth. She held him on her lap as he wiggled to get free. Her fingers explored his mouth, removing soggy bits of paper. "Hope I have a girl this time," she said. "Boys are so hard to handle."

Is she serious? Does she think girls won't get into things and stuff paper into their mouths?

A nurse wearing a white uniform and a lime-colored cardigan motioned to the young mother. She gathered up the kids, their coats and toys, and waddled after her.

⚖️ ⚖️ ⚖️

Aunt C stared into space. I nudged her. "You won't forget to ask him?"

"No, I won't," she said, in a flat voice.

The family hoped the autopsy report had arrived and we would finally know what caused his death. Aunt C said she would ask the doctor about the report. The newspapers, radio and TV kept saying Uncle Victor's death was probably suicide. The nearer the time came for The Committee to resume their hearings, the more stories there were about my uncle. No matter what anybody says, I'd never believe my uncle killed himself.

I tried to recall the doctor's face, but a lot about the day Uncle Victor died was shadowy, a bad dream.

While we waited, I looked through a stack of magazines and found a brochure about Dr. Harmon. There was a picture of him and his family. He looked like the movie star, Cary Grant! His wife was good looking too. There was a boy sitting between them who seemed about ten years old. He didn't look right. His head lolled forward and his mouth drooped open. The caption said the wife's name was Kathryn and the boy was called Davey.

There was a kid with palsy who rode the bus with us when I was in grade school. Some of the older boys were mean, calling him "retard," and they made him cry. He used a tricycle to steady himself because he staggered and dragged one leg as he walked. I talked to him, but he stuttered so much I couldn't understand him. But we tried anyway. One day, his mother thanked me for paying attention to him. She seemed very grateful. Dr. Harmon's son Davey looked a lot like that boy.

⚖️ ⚖️ ⚖️

Aunt C was twisting her handkerchief into a ball. One of her legs jumped up and down so I put my hand on her knee and it stopped bouncing. Finally, the nurse in the lime-colored sweater appeared and called Aunt C's name. We followed her down a hallway, past several exam rooms. She put us in one next to a door that opened to the main hallway. Cool air rushed in through the open transom and I could hear the elevators making their way up and down the building. I also thought doctors liked to have a rear entrance so you wouldn't know if they came in late or sneaked out.

It seemed like hours before there was a knock on the door. I swallowed hard when it opened and the doctor came into the exam room.

Harmon was tall, as I remembered, but he was even more handsome than the picture in the brochure. He smelled like Ipana toothpaste. When he smiled, his eyes crinkled around the corners.

He shook Aunt C's hand. "Celeste, always good to see you, but not under these circumstances."

"Thank you Carl. I think you know my niece, Josie."

"Oh yes, I remember," he replied. "I'm terribly sorry about Victor; he was a good man." He told us he heard Uncle Victor give a speech in New York years ago. "An excellent speaker, very passionate - raising money for a strike, I think."

Aunt C fidgeted on her perch at the end of an exam table; she looked like a bird ready to fly."

"How are you?" he asked.

"I'm pretty shaky," she said. "Maybe some more Milltown tranquilizers."

"Let's check your blood pressure. It was high last time." He attached the cuff around her arm, and squeezed the bulb, inflating the cuff with air. He placed the stethoscope against the inside of her arm as he listened and watched the meter on the wall. "Excellent," he said. "Your pressure is down."

"I need something to help me sleep."

"I have a few samples. I'll get them."

When he started for the door I interrupted, "Aunt C, isn't there something you wanted to ask him?"

"Oh - the report, the autopsy report," Aunt C said quietly.

Harmon looked surprised. "I thought we sent you a carbon copy."

"We haven't gotten anything," I told him.

"Let me check, perhaps it's on my desk.

When he reappeared he handed a small brown paper bag to Aunt C. "Samples," he explained. "I was mistaken, the coroner's report hasn't arrived. Look, I'll personally call the coroner's office to see if we can cut through the red tape."

"Thank you, Carl," Aunt C said, putting on her jacket.

"Anything else?" he asked.

Aunt C shook her head.

When we got to the waiting room I realized I had forgotten my purse in the exam room. "Back in a sec," I told Aunt C, and raced back to the waiting room. Dr. Harmon was still there, writing in my aunt's medical file.

"How can I help you?" he asked.

"Left my purse." Then I had an idea, and I thought it might be my only chance to talk to him alone. I took a deep breath I blurted it out, "Why did you say Uncle Victor died from an overdose?"

"I said, he might have died from an overdose." Harmon's eyes narrowed. "And, I said it because it's the truth."

The set of his mouth told me he was angry. He got up from his desk going to the window, his back to me.

"He never took pills! Everybody knows that." I raised my voice. "I know for a fact, he never saw you, Dr. Harmon. He said he hadn't been to see a doctor since they inducted him into the army, in the Second World War!"

Harmon wheeled around to face me. "You're right. I never treated Victor." The doctor no longer looked angry, only sad. He lowered his voice almost to a whisper, "I shouldn't tell you this, but under the circumstances, if you want to know about the sleeping pills, ask your aunt."

"Aunt Celeste?"

He nodded yes.

"I don't believe you!"

Our eyes locked; I waited for him to look away. Since he wasn't between me and the door I got up a little more courage. "I still think you're a liar." I ran out of the room, down the hallway, into the waiting room. I didn't say anything to Aunt C. I bolted out of the office and hurried to the elevators with Aunt C trying to keep up.

"What's going on?" she demanded.

"I'll tell you on the ride home."

In my haste to get to the elevators, I had bumped into a man standing by Harmon's private entrance. I was in such a hurry to get away from the doctor's office, I didn't get a good look at him. While we waited for the elevator, I watched the man open Harmon's private door and duck inside.

The door was the kind that locks automatically when closed, so he must have had a key. The man smelled like pipe tobacco, just like the FBI agent who came to the union hall when it was broken into and wrecked.

On the bus ride home, Aunt C kept looking in the small brown sack Dr. Harmon gave her. She shook her head in disappointment.

"What's wrong?"

"Nothing."

I tried to cheer her up, but no matter what I said, she stared out of the window; so I finally quit trying.

Aunt C looked through the sack again.

"Are those sleeping pills?" I asked.

"Some of them."

Dr. Harmon's comment came back like a punch in the head, "If you want to know about the sleeping pills, ask your aunt...." I had the oddest feeling, like the ground under the bus wasn't solid.

⚖ ⚖ ⚖

"Take a look at this, Grandpa." I showed him the brochure with the picture of Harmon and his family.

"Ahh, Doctor Harmon," Grandpa said, scrutinizing the picture. "Looks like Cary Grant. Handsome wife. Something off about the kid, though."

I told Grandpa about the visit with the doctor. "He had an answer for everything," I told him. Grandpa looked so worried, I was sorry I told him what Harmon said about Aunt C and the sleeping pills. But I knew if anyone could deal with it, it was Grandpa. When I was a little kid, I thought he knew everything. After I got older, I still thought he knew more than most people.

Grandpa must have spoken to Mom because, later, I overheard her and Goldie talking quietly about Aunt Celeste.

"Celeste said she started taking sleeping pills after the nightmares began," Mom told Goldie. "Harmon, wanted her to cut down, so she told him Victor needed them because he couldn't sleep, worrying about the hearings. In reality, they were for her."

"They used to give Milltown to the soldiers in the South Pacific," Goldie told her, "so they could stand the heat. They called them goof-balls; they're barbiturates. A lot of soldiers had to dry out, before they let them out of the service."

"What a mess," Mom said.

"It explains a lot," Goldie continued. "Maybe the doc is covering his ass because he passed out narcotics illegally."

"Do you think Celeste might have a problem using sleeping pills?"

Goldie didn't answer.

Chapter Eleven

Mom, Gramma, and McCloud were in the kitchen cooking. The place was a madhouse. The relatives from Idaho were expected any minute. We hadn't seen them for years.

McCloud stayed to help with the plans for the memorial. During the past several weeks it turned out he was a lot of help. Mom put him to work peeling potatoes while Gramma fried chicken and whipped up several cakes.

McCloud looked at the mound of potatoes. "I might as well be back in the army."

"Quit complaining," Mom told him. "No one's shooting at you."

Grandpa finished washing up the pots and pans and wiped his wet hands. "Gonna take a break," he said. He grabbed the cane resting next to the sink and limped out of the kitchen. I followed Grandpa to the porch. We sat on the porch swing, glad to be out of the hot kitchen.

"I guess Aunt C's still sleeping," I said. "Maybe she took too many happy pills."

"Happy pills?" Grandpa asked.

"You know, tranquilizers."

"Give her time," he said. "Maybe it'll be better after the memorial…."

Most of the time, Aunt C was sleeping or sitting quietly, staring into space; the "happy pills" weren't making her the least bit happy.

"When was the last time you saw the family from Idaho?" I asked.

"Last year, Christmas."

"What's Uncle Ray like?" Ray was Mom's brother.

"He looks like your Mom; some people thought they were twins."

"I mean as a person, Grandpa."

"Quiet, nose to the grindstone."

"And my cousins?"

"Junior? Good lookin' kid. Your age. The girls - twins, maybe eight years old, by now."

"Why don't we see them?"

He inhaled and the end of the cigarette glowed brighter. "Your grandma and I only see them once in a blue moon."

"Why didn't they visit us, Aunt C, Uncle Victor, Mom and me?"

"You'd have to ask your mom."

"Please Grandpa, tell me why."

He took another long drag on his cigarette. "Okay. Your ma and Ray had a falling-out when your father volunteered to fight in Spain."

"Is Uncle Ray a fascist? That's who my dad went to fight."

"No. No. It's not like that. The FBI visited him.

They threatened him and your ma. She was blacklisted and couldn't keep a job without the Feds showing up. Then, she got hired by that old guy who owns Goody's Bakery. Turns out, he fled Europe when Mussolini and the fascists came to power; he said he was sick of people pushing him around. When the FBI showed up and suggested he fire your mom, he told them he left Italy to get away from people like them."

"Gee whiz, Grandpa, that was a long time ago. Did Mom and Uncle Ray ever make up?"

He shrugged and took another drag on his cigarette. "You'll have to ask your mom."

⚖ ⚖ ⚖

When the family from Idaho arrived, I was as nervous as a cat on a tin roof. I wondered if I'd like them, or if they'd like me. I hoped we wouldn't all stand around looking at each other and nobody knowing what to say.

"That's them," Grandpa said. A blue 1950 Ford with a shiny bumper and chrome around the headlights pulled up in front of the house.

Two men got out. One was the spitting image of Mom: dark brown hair with gray streaks, like Mom's. The other, was a young-looking man, over six foot, followed by twin girls. A woman got out last, gathering up toys and helping the girls with their things.

Grandpa waved as they came up the walk. "That's Junior, with your uncle."

He was good looking. Junior looked about my age or a little older; too bad he was my first cousin.

The family from Idaho gave me the oddest feeling. They looked so familiar. I felt I should know them, but I didn't. We gathered in the kitchen for some drinks and food. Uncle Ray's voice sounded like Mom's and Aunt C's. Junior brushed his hair back from his face like me. We both did it at the same time and burst out laughing.

When the grown-ups started talking about the memorial we kids went to the living room. Cousin Ray inspected our record collection.

"Got any new stuff?" he asked, looking at Aunt C and Uncle Victor's collection of classical and folk music.

"I got all the latest," I bragged.

We left the twins engrossed in a game of Monopoly while we went upstairs to play records.

I put on a '78 of Lloyd Price's *Lawdy Miss Clawdy.* "All the kids are playing it at parties."

"We get one radio station at Applejack Junction. All it plays is cowboy music."

"This is R&B—Negro music. Everyone at high school listens to R&B. It's the newest thing."

"R&B?"

"Rhythm and Blues. There's only one program that plays R&B, a disc jockey named Bob Summerise. But the program comes on after 11:00 o'clock, so most school nights I can't hear it. What do you dance to?"

"In Applejack? Mostly swing and *Tuxedo Junction*, stuff like that."

"That's old, jitterbug music from the war. Do you know how to do the Bop?"

"What is it?"

"A dance, silly."

I put on the Clovers' *One Mint Julep* and showed him a few Bop steps. First, we walked slowly through the steps. Once he got the hang of it, we speeded things up. We played records and danced until Mom called us for supper.

After we finished eating, Mom and Uncle Ray told stories of when they were kids. Just as the twins were hustled off to bed my friend Jennie showed up. I swear, she has radar. She always knows when a cute guy shows up.

We went to my room and Jennie took over giving Junior more dance lessons. She was the one who taught me. Jennie could dance. I mean dance, dance. She took center stage when we went to the Trianon Ballroom, and at every house party. She could mimic her partners' steps and make them look a thousand times better. It didn't hurt that she had the biggest dimples and flaming red hair, shiny like copper. The boys always fell for that. Some catty girls said it was dyed, but every hair on her body matched. For a while, I used a rinse and colored mine red; some kids at school thought mine was real and hers was fake! It ticked her off a lot, so I washed the color out.

Ray had a blast dancing with Jennie. He couldn't take his eyes off her. He was a goner.

Mom told us to call it a night. We had to get up early to get ready for the memorial. Jennie put on her coat and gave Junior a hug. His face turned red, but he had the biggest grin. After she was out of earshot, he said, "Your friend is a doll."

Junior and I kept talking; neither one of us was sleepy.

"Joz, why didn't we ever see each other when were little kids?" he asked.

I started to laugh. "I asked the same thing."

"I was mad about it, but I didn't know who to be mad at."

"Try the Feds," I suggested.

He didn't have a clue what I was talking about. I told him about my Dad going to Spain and how Mom was blacklisted. I asked him if he knew the FBI paid a visit to his dad around that time. He shook his head "no," but he had a funny look on his face.

Mom told us again to hit the hay. This time it sounded like she meant it.

Junior started out of the door and stopped, "I want the low-down; I want to hear about everything."

I promised I would tell him about it in the morning, and he left to go to sleep downstairs. As I brushed my hair, getting ready for bed, I thought about how cool Junior was. We were on the same wavelength. I wondered how families could drift so far apart. Well, at least they were here now.

Chapter Twelve

It was the day of the memorial and we still hadn't gotten the autopsy report. More and more rumors floated around, saying Uncle Victor's death was a suicide. The night before the memorial, Goldie and Anthony Avilá came to the house.

"The union secretary wrote a letter asking the autopsy report be released to the Victor Jenkins family," Goldie told us.

"So did the cannery workers union," Avilá added.

"We could send a contingent to meet with the coroner's office," Goldie suggested. "It might pressure them."

They told us they thought the coroner's office was holding up the report on purpose.

It upset me terribly that people might think he had killed himself, but I felt a little better knowing there were other people willing to help us.

⚖ ⚖ ⚖

I was worried I might break down at the memorial. If tears started, I might not be able to stop. When we arrived at the union hall for the memorial we found it filled with flowers. Union members had done most of the work. Red roses and white carnations perfumed the air.

Many pictures of Uncle Victor were hanging on the wall. I thought I knew everything about him, but I was surprised to see photographs from his army days and several medals. I had no idea he served in North Africa and Europe during the war. Uncle Victor called it "the big war." He started calling it that after the Korean war broke out. I got a lump in my throat when I saw him in his uniform, standing with his buddies in front of a jeep all of them smiling. I couldn't help thinking he survived one war only to fight another at home. He said the fight with the employers was a class war.

As people arrived, Grandpa greeted old friends. Gramma never let Aunt C out of her sight. Aunt C stared into space. She wore her hair in a French roll, plain dark suit and pumps and a red carnation in the lapel. She had gulped down several "happy pills" as she applied make-up earlier in the morning. On the outside she looked good; inside she must have been a wreck. Grandpa said that maybe she would get better once the memorial was over.

Gramma worried about her too. She always made a fuss over us kids, but now she barely noticed my cousins or me. She spent all her time hovering over Aunt C.

Once the hall filled and everyone was seated, a young couple stood at the front of the room waiting for the audience to quiet down. The woman had a guitar and the man a harmonica. When the only sound was a single muffled cough and the distant hum of traffic from the street faded, they played Joe Hill. They played it slowly, just the music, no words. I said the words to myself.

I dreamed I saw Joe Hill last night,
"Alive as you and me. "But Joe," I said
"You're ten years dead."
"I never died," said he.
"I never died," said he.

As the music played, I imagined an old-fashioned wagon, pulled by four white horses, like something from the Civil War days. There was a casket on the wagon and a drummer leading the way to a cemetery on a hill. Even though it was sad, somehow the music and the picture in my mind seemed beautiful.

As president of the union, Goldie welcomed everyone and talked about Uncle Victor as a leader and organizer, and his friend. He introduced Anthony Avilá as a spokesman for the Cannery Workers' Union. Then Goldie invited the audience to stand and speak about Victor's life. One by one, people told stories about him. Some were funny, others sad.

A heavy-set woman in a purple dress spoke. "I'm not a union member, and I'm not used to giving speeches, but I have something to say." Her voice quavered as she told how Uncle Victor came to her house during a strike. When he discovered just one can of green beans in the cupboard, he insisted the family come and stay with him and Celeste. She pointed to Aunt C. "That's Victor's wife, Mrs. Jenkins. Right over there. You couldn't ask for better people."

There were lots of stories like that. Uncle Ray stood up. My cousin Junior and I looked at each other in surprise. "Victor Jenkins was my brother-in-law. You couldn't ask for a better person. I'm proud to have known him and have him as part of my family."

Mom started to cry. So did I. Even Grandpa looked like he might tear up.

After everyone finished speaking, the two musicians returned to the front of the hall. The woman sang *The Rebel Girl*. It was Uncle Victor's favorite song. The hair on my arms stood up. He always said it reminded him of Aunt C. It was almost like he was saying goodbye to her.

There are women of many descriptions
In this queer world, as everyone knows.
Some are living in beautiful mansions,
And are wearing the finest of clothes.
There are blue-blooded queens and princesses,
Who have charms made of diamonds and pearl;
But the only and thoroughbred lady
Is the Rebel Girl.

When the memorial ended, we stood and sang *Solidarity Forever*. It sounded more like we were in church than a union hall. Everyone sang with such feeling it made me feel like we were all one family.

⚖ ⚖ ⚖

Two of Uncle Victor's distant relatives left abruptly after the memorial. Uncle Victor's great aunt had been shaking her head in disapproval when people got up to speak. She had sharp features and a constant frown that made her look even more disapproving. I wondered what she would think about dancing, playing cards or having any kind of fun. I'm sure she would have looked at all those things as dangerous for your health. I was glad the family from Uncle Victor's side didn't come to the house.

The relatives from Idaho also seemed a little shocked at the memorial, but they didn't disappear like the other ones.

"Interesting gathering," Uncle Ray said to Grandpa when we got back to the house. "Never saw anything like it before."

"How's that?" Grandpa asked.

"Usually, a minister addresses the crowd and maybe someone from the family reads a poem or something like that, then there are prayers."

"There was a minister," Grandpa said. "Old Reverend Corywicks."

"He didn't preach," Ray argued. "He talked about Victor being an organizer and carrying on his work."

"So?"

"I didn't say I didn't like it; it's just different. Real different," he mumbled.

"Speak up, couldn't hear you."

"Never mind, Dad."

⚖ ⚖ ⚖

When the conversation got edgy between Grandpa and Uncle Ray, Junior and I went to my room to play records. I put on a Clovers' record. He plopped himself down on the floor, back against the wall, while I sat cross-legged on the bed.

"Whatcha think?" I asked. "About the memorial?"

Junior shrugged. "Beats all that preachin'. I was glad Dad said something." He was quiet for a moment then said, "Joz, I want to ask you something...."

Here it comes - the big question - bet a million dollars.

"Was Uncle Victor a Communist?"

And there it was. I'd wondered how long it was going to take him. "It's illegal for him to be a Communist and hold office in a union," I said.

"You can tell me; I won't say anything."

"He didn't belong, but I think some of his ideas were the same."

"Hmm." He sat quietly for a while then asked, "Exactly what is a Communist? I know it's supposed to be something bad. That's what the newspapers and Junior Scholastic say. But Uncle Victor was a good guy."

"Yeah, he was. A real good one."

"If he wasn't a Communist, why was The Committee after him?"

"There are a lot of Communists in the union he worked for. Uncle Victor said they were the best guys. Aunt C is a party member. Mom was. Our Grandpa is a Socialist.

"I didn't know that."

"Doesn't your dad tell you anything?"

"We talk a lot. Dad isn't interested in politics. I don't understand. What was Uncle Victor doing that was so terrible?"

"He wasn't doing anything wrong. You know all that stuff in the papers about Communists being foreign agents? That's all crap. They had meetings here at the house sometimes; and if you want to know the truth, they were boring. All they ever talked about was history and economics and junk like that. The good stuff were things like picketing Safeway for not hiring Negroes. I went on those picket lines myself."

"Just curious," he explained. Then he got quiet again.

Now what? He had already asked the sixty-four-dollar question.

"Uncle Victor came to visit us a couple years ago."

"In Idaho? He never said."

"He was in Pocatello for a union conference and dropped by to see Dad on the spur of the moment. A few days afterwards a couple of FBI agents came to the house. They asked Dad to tell them everything he knew about Uncle Victor's union activity and to report to them."

"They asked him to be a stool pigeon?"

"Dad would never fink on anyone!" There was another long silence. "But he did ask Uncle Victor not to come around for a while." Junior looked real upset.

"It's all right," I told him.

"You don't understand." He said, "There's more. Dad got hurt right after that and couldn't work and Uncle Victor and Aunt C sent us money. A guy would stop by every few weeks with money in an envelope. Uncle Victor didn't want to send it in the mail because he was afraid the Feds would cause trouble for Dad." Junior was quiet again, then said, "I was ashamed that Dad told him not to come to our house and then Uncle Victor helped us out anyway."

I felt tears starting. That was my Uncle Victor to a tee. "Don't feel bad, Junior; Uncle Victor knew all about how dirty the Feds are. He never would have blamed Uncle Ray, never."

⚖️ ⚖️ ⚖️

The next day Junior and the rest of his family packed-up their car for the trip back to Idaho. "Wish you could stay longer," I told him.

"You'll see me real soon," he said. "I love Seattle."

"Maybe you'd love to see my friend Jennie too?"

"I might." A grin spread across his face. "I'll miss you too, Joz." He lowered his voice so the rest of the family couldn't hear, "Watch out for those three-letter guys."

"The FBI?"

He nodded. "I wish they'd visit us again — I'd tell them to go to hell!"

Chapter Thirteen

After the memorial Mom thought I should try going back to school. I was walking out of the door when I spotted a letter for me on the little table next to the door. My heart raced when I saw the foreign stamp. But I was surprised to see it was from Alain's mother, Tamara. The letter read:

> Dear Josette:
>
> Alain was unable to reach you by telephone to convey our condolences on the loss of your uncle, Victor Jenkins. There was a short article in the newspaper, Le Monde, reporting his death and referencing his work organizing support for a world-wide union protest against apartheid in South Africa. My son was most enthusiastic about meeting him and your family during his brief stay in Seattle. Alain said he will try to reach you again; in the meantime, please know our thoughts are with you. Victor Jenkins will be missed by many.
>
> Sincerely, Tamara Fournier

I thought the note from her was grand, and Aunt C and Mom liked it a lot. It made me feel better because I knew Alain hadn't forgotten me. The day after Mrs. Fornier's letter came, a telegram arrived from Alain. It read: DEAR JOSETTE: STOP. MY HEART IS WITH YOU. STOP. LOVE. ALAIN.

I read and re-read the telegram. It was the first telegram I had ever gotten and couldn't quit looking at the yellow piece of paper with the odd lettering. The words "My heart is with you" kept jumping off the page. That night, I folded the telegram and put it under my pillow, just as I had done when I was a little kid with things I thought magical.

⚖ ⚖ ⚖

A few days after I got the telegram, Mom called me to the telephone. "Josie, long distance. There's an international operator on the line."

The operator said, "Alain Fournier calling from Haiti. Is this Josette Thompson?"

"Josette?" Alain asked.

"Alain! Wow! You're in Haiti?"

"Can't talk long. I'll call you when we get into New York. Are you..."

There was a lot of static on the line and it went dead.

"What did he say?" Mom asked.

"The line went dead. He's in Haiti and he said he'd call when he got to New York."

I guess I must have looked sad because Mom asked me what was wrong.

"He didn't say when he was going to get to New York."

Funny how you can be up one minute and down the next.

Chapter Fourteen

I stopped at the Star Drugs to pickup notebook paper for school. Alain was all I could think about. I either dreamed about him at night, or found myself day-dreaming about him, so I didn't notice when a pimple-faced kid followed me out of the drugstore. On the way to the bus stop, he got close and reached out to touch my breast.

Now this wasn't the first time this had happened, and I was ready for him. He appeared to be around 14 or 15 years old. I shouted at him, "Oh, you're in the tit-feeling stage! Make you feel like a big man?"

People on the street stopped, and turned to stare. His face got red but he reached to try his luck again. "Don't even try it," I told him. I pulled my foot back to give him a good kick. Before I could get a good kick-in, a car screeched to a stop beside us.

"Get the hell away from her," Agent Brock hollered.

The kid argued until the agent flashed his badge. "You want me to arrest you?"

The kid raced away down the sidewalk.

"I can take care of myself," I told Brock. It ticked me off. I was making mincemeat of that pimple faced goof-ball. I was more upset seeing that Brock and his buddy were still hanging around the neighborhood than I was about the kid.

"You're welcome," the agent said, sarcasm dripping from each word. *Why was the FBI still hanging around? What did they want now?*

⚖ ⚖ ⚖

When I got home, Aunt C was sleeping. I didn't want to wake her, but was dying to talk to someone. I felt fidgety, not about the dumbo kid, but about having the agent act like he was the big hero saving me, pretending to be my friend.

Luckily for me, Goldie stopped by to check on Aunt C, so there was someone to talk to about running into the agent.

"Do you believe in coincidences?" I asked.

"Not when it comes to those jokers," he said. "The FBI was around a couple of days ago, talking with Celeste."

"Really? She didn't tell me."

"Agent Brock asked her out for coffee."

"You gotta be kidding."

"Then he showed up yesterday morning when she went out for the newspaper."

"Nobody ever tells me anything," I complained.

"She doesn't want you to worry. I asked McCloud to come down for a few days, to keep an eye on things."

"Does Mom know? They don't always get along."

"Her idea."

"Hmm. Why didn't she ask you?"

"I'm traveling for the union the rest of the month. McCloud's coming tonight."

⚖ ⚖ ⚖

Mom said supper would be late; she wanted to wait until McCloud arrived. I was in the middle of a Nero Wolfe mystery when my nose started twitching. I tried to guess what we were having for dinner. I made myself a bet it was fried chicken and lemon chiffon pie. If I was wrong, I told myself I would stay off the phone for the rest of the evening. Usually I called Jennie and we talked a marathon.

When I got to the kitchen, Aunt C, Goldie and McCloud were at the table. McCloud was wearing his Sunday best, which was a pair of blue jeans and a clean white dress shirt, top two buttons undone and sleeves rolled up with a pack of Pall Malls stuck in one side. He still smelled like sawdust.

"Wow! What's the occasion?" I asked, when I saw the platter of fried chicken and a pie cooling on the counter.

"No occasion," Mom said. "We deserve a treat, now and then."

"Hey, McCloud," I punched his shoulder, "What you dressed up for?"

"Tryin' to look like a city slicker," he answered.

"Needs more work. And, you need a haircut."

He laughed. "My dad threatened to buy me a dog collar when it got long." He ran his fingers through his hair.

The food was wonderful, but more than anything it was neat to be together. It was almost like it had been when Uncle Victor was alive.

"How long are you staying?"

"It's up to your ma."

"A while," she said. "I'm going back to work, Joz."

"Not already," I protested.

"Josie, it's been a month. I can lose my job if I don't go back. The old man at Goody's Bakery has been calling, whining about how he needs me."

"I wish it was longer," I told her.

"We need the money," she said.

After the table was cleared, Mom and Aunt C served coffee and pie.

"Boy, it's hot in here," Aunt C said, opening the back door.

"Summer weather, early this year," Mom remarked.

"That's why I got the time off," McCloud said, "Its too dry. Too big a chance for a forest fire. No logs in reserve so the mill shut down."

"When do you go back to work?" I asked Mom.

"Tomorrow night."

⚖️ ⚖️ ⚖️

After supper, Goldie showed up and he and McCloud told stories about when they were young, and kidded Mom and Aunt C about high school. When they told one about Uncle Victor, Aunt C excused herself, saying she was tired, and went to the bedroom. She took a cocktail with her.

"You can have the spare room, if that's okay," Mom told McCloud. "Or the couch, if you prefer."

"Spare room's fine," he said.

It was the room where Uncle Victor passed away, and I was surprised he said he would stay there. But McCloud was full of surprises. Just when you expected him to act goofy, he was serious. You never knew what he would do.

"Guess I'll put my gear away," McCloud said, heading to the spare room with a duffel bag.

"I better say goodnight, too," Goldie said. "Got an early train tomorrow."

"When are you coming back?" Mom asked.

"A couple of weeks."

"I'll walk you to your car," she said.

Goldie and Mom had been going out for a long time. They never said anything to me, but I could tell they were pretty serious about each other. He was at the house whenever she was off work.

⚖ ⚖ ⚖

For days after the memorial, Aunt C looked bedraggled. She wasn't fixing her hair; she slept a lot, and still wasn't talking much. She was having a few more drinks each night after dinner. One beautiful day I convinced her to go to the Vesuvius with me for lunch. It was warm, not a cloud in the sky, and you could see Mount Rainier in the distance. Puget Sound sparkled in the sun. There was no place on earth like the Pacific Northwest on a sunny day.

When we got to the market, tourists were gathered, as usual, for the world famous fish toss. To our surprise, we found a line to get into the Vesuvius. One of the best-kept secrets in Seattle was no longer a secret.

It looked like we were in for a wait and I needed to go to the restroom, so I told Aunt C I would meet her inside the restaurant. I made my way back through the crowd. When I got to the public bathroom, I found a couple of men lounging outside. They smelled of alcohol and their leathery skin said they were on the bum.

"Can you ssshhhpare a buck?" a man dressed in a plaid shirt asked. He bobbed around like a puppet on a string.

"Sorry," I said, not wanting to take my wallet out of my jeans in front of the men.

He cursed me. I ignored him and went into the women's. The men weren't scary; they were so drunk, a little push would have knocked them down. On the way back to join Aunt C, Mrs. Fujimoto motioned me to her vegetable stall.

She gave me a hug and asked about everyone. Each question was followed with an apology because she hadn't been able to attend Uncle Victor's memorial. It seemed as if our conversation took forever, and I was anxious to get back to Aunt C.

When I finally got back to the restaurant, the line was gone and Aunt C was at a table in the rear. I was surprised to see a man sitting with her. His back was to me. He was dressed in a suit, had brown hair with a bald spot showing. When I got closer, I noticed the sweet smell of pipe tobacco. I was pretty sure I knew who it was.

Aunt C stared at the table, not looking at the man.

"Think about it, Mrs. Jenkins. I can help," he said.

The man reached for his hat, and when he stood up and turned around, I was face-to-face with Agent Brock. After he put on his hat, he twisted the brim around until he had it just so. He stared with blue eyes that glistened.

"My card," he said, handing one to me.

"Not pleased, I'm sure," I said handing it back. He tipped his hat to Aunt C and brushed past me.

"Take it easy, kid," he said. "Don't take any wooden nickels."

⚖ ⚖ ⚖

"What the heck, Aunt C?"

"He said he wants to be my friend."

"That's nuts!"

"Yeech," she said, like she had a bad taste in her mouth.

"Still want lunch?"

"I lost my appetite."

We decided to have some tea and pastry instead of lunch. We didn't see our regular waiter. In his place was a young woman wearing a short skirt and high spike heels that clicked when she walked. I noticed Aunt C's hands were shaking when she drank her tea.

"What else did Brock say?" I asked.

"The oddest thing. He said he could smooth everything over. When I asked him like what, he smiled - like he had a big secret."

⚖ ⚖ ⚖

After we got home, I discovered there was more to the story when Aunt C told Mom and McCloud about our lunch being crashed by the agent. "Josie went to the rest room and Brock walked right up to the table and sat down. His partner was nowhere in sight. I thought it was odd because agents always travel in pairs. I asked him where his partner was. My partner isn't involved in this, he said. Then he told me some jazz about admiring me for a long time."

Mom asked, "Did he say anything else that might give us a clue?"

"It was implied that there's trouble brewing, and if I'm his friend, everything will be hunky-dory."

"Don't believe it," McCloud said. "A rat is always a rat."

"I think the guy is kind of off," Aunt C told McCloud. "His eyes got all shiny and he kept looking around, nervous-like."

"That's it," McCloud said. "You need someone with you from now on."

"All the time?" Aunt C asked.

"All the time," Mom told her.

"Or until we know the score," McCloud said.

Chapter Fifteen

"Josie, phone call. Hurry!" Mom held the phone out to me, and motioned to hurry. "It's from New York."

I grabbed the phone. "Alain?"

"Finally made it," he said. His voice sounded like he was talking in a tin can.

It had been almost ten days since he phoned from Haiti. "We are in New York. We ran into a little weather," he explained. "It took a little longer to get here than I thought."

"What were you guys doing in Haiti?"

"The usual, business for the fat cats. Forget about that. How are you? And your mom and your aunt?"

"It's been hard, but we're okay."

"Did you get the package?"

"Mom, did we get a package from Alain?"

She shook her head.

"Tamara's sending it. It should be there soon," he said.

83

I thought it was kind of unusual for a kid to call their parent by their first name, but I had run into other people who did it.

"Is your ship ever coming back here?" I asked hopefully.

"We never know where they'll send us. I thought about hopping a train or bus to see you, but by the time I got there I'd have to turn around and go back. Flying is way too expensive."

"Maybe next time," I said without conviction.

"Maybe next time."

There was a long pause. "I'll figure out something," he said.

"Maybe I'll make a trip to France," I said, dreaming.

"Please write, Joz."

I promised I would. He understood I hadn't felt like writing after Uncle Victor died. I not only didn't feel like writing to him, for a long time I hadn't felt like doing much of anything.

The operator broke in, saying his time was up. "I'll write," he said. Take care of yourself and…."

The connection was broken. I listened to the sound of the phone buzzing for a few seconds. Finally, I put the receiver back on the hook.

"What did he say?" Mom asked.

"Nothing," I said. God, it was nice to hear his voice. I wondered what he was going to say when we got cutoff. Maybe, "I love you?" I knew it was silly, but I pretended he said it.

I went to my room intending to write him a letter but lay on the bed instead, dreaming about the day I met him and the night he kissed me.

Chapter Sixteen

My favorite chair was the Morris chair. You can snuggle and relax. I liked to read sitting in that chair. We'd had it ever since I could remember, and sometimes I liked to sit in it and just look around the room. Uncle Victor had made book shelves out of bricks and unfinished planks. We had every kind of book, from auto repair to *Gray's Anatomy* and Will Durant's *The Story of Civilization*. Myself, I was a big fan of Rex Stout's Nero Wolfe detective stories.

Aunt C's paintings were on the walls. She painted people doing ordinary things, like women talking over a fence, an old lady sweeping, or a little boy playing with blocks.

When my aunt and uncle bought the house, it was a wreck. They worked on it every spare moment. They laid down a hardwood floor in the living room. After it was stained, they gave me a pair of heavy woolen socks, let me invite some kids from the neighborhood, and we skated across the floor to buff the many coats of wax Uncle Victor had applied.

The best thing was the fireplace. I liked winter when the fireplace was lit and we would sit drinking hot chocolate and telling stories, or just watching the bits of pitch in the logs sizzle and explode.

As they were fixing up the house, Uncle Victor discovered a beautiful wood mantel under a thick coat of green paint. Aunt C wanted to paint over the green with crimson and black, but Uncle Victor started scraping and sanding until he got down to the wood. It was Birdseye Maple. After it was stained, varnished and sanded a zillion times, it glistened like fat in the bottom of a roasting pan. Sometimes I liked to sit in the Morris chair and look at the fireplace, even when there was no fire. An old Seth Thomas clock was on the mantel. It chimed on the hour and the half hour. There were two photographs: one of Aunt C's and Uncle Victor's wedding, and a baby picture of me.

⚖ ⚖ ⚖

The snack bar on East Madison Street was packed. Even so, it was easy to find Jennie. Look for red hair and a pile of boys milling around. We got a booth in the back room where it wasn't so crowded. The hours flew by while we caught up. We talked and poured quarters into the juke box. I think we played *Night Train* a hundred times. Finally, some customers yelled at us, "Enough is enough!" It was getting late, so we said goodbye. It felt good doing normal things. I found myself humming, all the way home.

It was almost time for supper. I opened the door expecting to smell food cooking. Instead, there was a heavy odor of paint.

Aunt C crouched in front of the fireplace, newspapers spread around her. The Seth Thomas clock and the photographs were gone. The mantel was now bright red. She was painting its trim black.

"Aunt C, what are you doing?" I wanted to cry, seeing Uncle Victors wood mantle covered with paint.

"I wanted to do this for a long time," she said.

She sounded angry. When I got closer, I saw her hair was not combed. She had wrapped a scarf around it to keep it up and out of her face. She was wearing the same clothes she had worn the day before. I went to the kitchen and found Mom drinking coffee and staring out of the window.

"What is she doing?" I demanded.

She motioned me to sit.

"She's acting nuts," I said. A tear, slid down my cheek.

Aunt Celeste cursed loudly and burst through the double doors.

"Tipped the paint over," she said.

She held up a brush. Her fingers were covered with black paint. She had a can of turpentine in the other hand and went to the laundry room. After she cleaned up, she went straight back to the living room without a word. I peeked through the double doors and found her finishing up the edges around the mantel.

Tears started again, and Mom reached out to take my hand.

"She's grieving," she explained.

"By destroying something? Something Uncle Victor made?"

"She's angry. You know she misses him terribly."

"That's a bizarre way to show it."

"Everyone has their own way; dealing with death is very difficult."

"I wish she hadn't done it. I think about Uncle Victor every time I look at the fireplace."

"Maybe that's why she did it," she suggested. Maybe it reminds her of him too much."

What Mom said sounded right, but she didn't see the gleam in Aunt C's eyes, and I couldn't forget that look.

Chapter Seventeen

One morning after Mom went back to work, I expected to find the kitchen empty. To my surprise, McCloud was busy peeling potatoes.

"Morning, Josie. Give me a hand, will ya?"

"You can cook?"

"Have to, your ma said so," he said with a grin.

He handed me a peeler and we finished the job together.

"Left in the eyes," I pointed out.

"Boy! Just like your ma."

"Thank you."

"Picky."

"We aren't picky - we do good work," I retorted.

"Picky and bossy."

"Just cook, if you can."

"Ha!" he said.

I was glad McCloud was going to stick around for awhile. He and Aunt C were real close. Maybe he could talk some sense into her about Dr. Harmon - and taking so many happy pills.

We had just sat down to eat when there was a tap on the back door. McCloud opened the door to a middle-aged man wearing a suit a couple of sizes too large. He was holding a clip board and some papers. The man smiled, but it seemed fake. The minute I saw him, I got that feeling, the one you get when something isn't quite right but you aren't sure what it is.

"Are you A.R. McCloud?"

Before McCloud could answer the man threw a paper at McCloud; it floated to the floor. "You've been served," he cried and rushed down the steps, two at a time.

McCloud picked up the paper and found a ten-dollar bill clipped to it. He stuffed the money into his shirt pocket and leaped down the full flight of steps after the process server. He caught up with him before he got to his car. McCloud gave him a shove and the guy went flying, landing face down on the grassy parking strip. He pulled his arms up to cover his head. "Don't hurt me," he whimpered.

McCloud turned the man over and grabbed him by the collar. He jerked the process server to his feet.

"Look at me," McCloud said.

He kept looking at the ground.

McCloud stuffed the ten-dollar bill into the breast pocket of the man's suit jacket.

"Forgot your fee," he said, making a face. Then McCloud brushed off the man's jacket, and turned him so he faced his car. The man jerked open the door, climbed in and started the engine. We watched him speed down the street.

On the way to the house McCloud wore a big smile. "I think we scared the bejesus out of him."

"He deserved it."

We looked at the paper from the server. I had seen one like it before, when Uncle Victor was subpoenaed by The Committee. The paper was typed with a typewriter that left black dots in the "o"s. It looked like something from a first year high school typing class. The paper ordered McCloud to appear in thirty days.

I asked him what he was going to do when he appeared before The Committee.

"Darned if I know. Take the fifth, I guess."

"Why don't you talk to Goldie the next time he phones," I said, worried. "He and Uncle Victor talked a lot about the hearings.

⚖   ⚖   ⚖

It wasn't long after the process server left when Mom arrived home.

"You're early. Something happen at work?" I asked.

"I got subpoenaed."

"You, too?" McCloud asked.

"And laid off," she added.

"What? No! Mom, after all these years Old man Goody fires you?"

"Not fired, Josie, laid off. That means I can collect my rocking chair."

"Your what?"

"Unemployment compensation."

"But old man Goody defended you when the FBI visited him," I argued. I was shaken but tried to hide it.

"Things are different now. My name and where I work will be in the papers. Actually, he said he'd hire me back when things cooled down. We need to be quiet about that."

She looked tired. "Can I get you something? A cup of coffee?"

"Thanks, sweetheart. That would be real nice. Think I'll rest these dogs too." She removed her shoes and put her feet up on the couch. Even after two cups of coffee, she fell asleep.

McCloud and I went to the kitchen so we wouldn't wake her.

"Why do you think they subpoenaed Mom? She's not involved in politics."

"Hard to tell what reason The Committee has. Maybe her past. Maybe who she's related to."

I filled McCloud's cup with fresh coffee and got a glass of milk for myself.

"Thanks, Josie," he said sipping the hot liquid. "I think The Committee still insists on putting Victor on trial. They might try to smear him and the union by subpoenaing relatives and friends."

"Why not Aunt C, then?"

"They can't make her testify about him, and it wouldn't look good. He just died, and now she's a widow. That's pretty heartless, even for The Committee."

⚖️ ⚖️ ⚖️

We were still talking about The Committee when Aunt C joined us. "What's going on? Why is Terry home from work?"

"Mom and McCloud got subpoenaed."

"Now it all makes sense."

"What makes sense?"

"The day Agent Brock crashed our lunch at the Vesuvius. He kept hinting about something big happening, that he could take care of, if I was nice to him. He must have meant the hearings."

McCloud slid his chair back so fast it made a loud squeaking sound. He started pacing around the kitchen, looking like he wanted to hit something. Finally he said, "Son-of-a-bitch."

Aunt C didn't act upset, but later she went to her bedroom and didn't join us for supper. She only came out of her room a couple of times to mix up a cocktail.

⚖️ ⚖️ ⚖️

I asked Mom if she planned on hiring a lawyer.

"With what money?" she asked.

She said she decided to volunteer for the defense committee. "Especially now that I need some defending," she laughed bitterly. "Beats working."

"It'll be just your luck the employment office will find a job for you," McCloud told her.

"Bite your tongue."

"Even if they do," I said, "you'll get fired when the FBI shows up."

⚖️ ⚖️ ⚖️

Later in the evening, I heard Mom talking to Goldie long distance. He was still in San Francisco on union business. She acted like getting the subpoena wasn't anything, but she sounded anxious and kept asking him when he was going to come home.

Aunt C was at the writing desk opening mail.

"Look at this," she said holding up an envelope. It's addressed to Mr. and Mrs. Jenkins and the return address is the union office.

"How strange," I said. "Everyone at the union knows Uncle Victor died."

She read the letter and tears welled up in her eyes.

"What?" I cried, grabbing the letter from her. It looked like a Xeroxed copy of a typed report. It had spelling errors. It read: "Janury 23, 1954 Minutes of club meeting. Eight members present for waterfront branch meeting. Memburs diskuss need for secretcy. Them wants Jenkins to admit his membership. He refuses, slams fist on tabel. Says he won't go to jail, he will name names. Jenkins looks scared and leeves."

"This is crazy," Aunt C said.

"This is one of those letters Mom told us about," I explained. "The defense committee said everyone who got subpoenaed is getting anonymous letters."

"The letter makes it sound like he's in a secret meeting and scared to death," she said, wiping tears away. "Maybe scared enough to commit suicide."

"Mom thinks it might be done to frighten people, make them think the Feds are everywhere."

"It makes me feel like there's an informant under every rock," Aunt C said.

"Who would do this?" I asked.

At the end of the evening we agreed it could be someone like Agent Brock, or even Brock and his partner.

⚖ ⚖ ⚖

A few nights later, Aunt C and I had the house to ourselves. Mom had gone to a defense committee meeting and McCloud was off to who-knew-where. The weather had gotten warmer and stayed warm into the evening. Neither of us felt like eating a big meal, so we made sandwiches and had root beer floats for dessert. Afterwards we played Scrabble.

"Really Aunt C? Zoeae, for 48 points? What does that even mean?"

"Look it up. It's legit."

We didn't play long. Aunt C wanted to hit the hay, so I checked to make sure the doors and windows were locked and put out the lights, just as McCloud had instructed.

I was upstairs, reading a new book by Daphne du Maurier, *My Cousin Rachel*, when my bedroom door slowly opened. Aunt C stood in the doorway with her finger to her lips. "There's someone outside the house," she whispered. "Under my bedroom window. Listen...."

A voice called Aunt C's name. "Cel - eh - este. Cel - eh - este. It kept calling her name, over and over.

"We need something," she whispered, picking up a heavy doorstop shaped like a cat. I found an old baseball bat in the back of my closet. We snuck down the darkened hallway and sat at the top of the stairs. The voice kept calling and calling.

It seemed like hours before the voice stopped. Then there was laughter and we heard a car drive away. It was quiet for a long time before we went downstairs. The windows and doors were still locked. No one had gotten in. We sat huddled together in the living room, waiting for McCloud or Mom to come home. I was still clutching the baseball bat when the doorknob rattled.

"Who is it?" Aunt C asked.

"It's me."

The door opened and I swung the bat. McCloud stepped in. He managed to sidestep before he got hit. Aunt C was still standing with the metal cat doorstop raised above her head.

"Whoa," he said. "What's goin' on?"

"We had visitors," Aunt C said, "and I almost hit you." Tears formed in her eyes.

"Okay, okay," he said. He put his arms around her. "And put that bat away will you?" he said to me.

About the time we finished filling him in, Mom arrived. While we told Terry the story, McCloud disappeared outside.

I thought he went to check if everything was okay, but he came back with something in his jacket. He pulled a pistol from his pocket. "It's a forty-five automatic," he said. "I kept it when I got mustered out of the army."

"Jesus, McCloud!" Terry exclaimed.

"Celeste, if anyone tries to get in here, I want you to fire through the door," he instructed. He showed her how the gun worked and where the safety catch was.

"Put that thing away." Terry glared at him. "Where were you?" she demanded. "You insisted Celeste needed someone with her all the time. Where were you?"

McCloud looked at the rug. "I just went to shoot a couple quick games of pool."

"You smell like a brewery," Terry said.

"It won't happen again."

⚖ ⚖ ⚖

McCloud got up late the next morning. He went straight to the kitchen where Mom was preparing lunch. I couldn't hear what they said, but he looked happy when he came into the living room.

"Hey, Josie, what'cha readin'?" McCloud asked, making himself comfortable in the Morris chair.

"Uncle Victor's union paper, Speak Out." I was reading an article about the Rosenbergs in it. "Golly, McCloud, look at this picture of Ethel. She has such sad eyes. You think they might really give her the chair?"

McCloud shook his head. "Nothing surprises me anymore."

"It doesn't look like she did anything. Her brother is saving his own behind, ratting on his sister."

"The powers-that-be are upping the ante. This so-called spy ring," McCloud said. "We're losing in Korea, the Chinese and the North Koreans are beating the crap out of the U.S."

"What's that got to do with the Rosenbergs?"

"It's a way to scare the hell out of people, paint radicals as spies, saboteurs, something foreign. In this case, it might be to justify the use of the atomic bomb in the war; and the whole climate is putting the brakes on the unions."

I had gone to a demonstration to free Ethel Rosenberg and her husband; it was real scary, but I'd go again. I looked at the picture of Ethel once more, "See her eyes. I bet she's thinking about her little boys."

⚖ ⚖ ⚖

The night after we heard voices under Aunt C's window, we started getting crank phone calls. When I answered a loud sound blasted over the receiver that almost broke my eardrum. There was cursing, stuff I wouldn't repeat.

94

According to Mom, everyone who was subpoenaed was getting crank calls and night visitors, too.

"Why don't you get an unlisted phone number?" McCloud suggested.

"Doesn't help; the calls start up a few days later," Mom told him.

"Has ta be the Feds or cops," McCloud guessed. "They're the only ones that could get unlisted numbers so quickly."

I started answering the phone holding it away from my ear. One night there were so many calls I took the phone off the hook, but a loud buzzing started a minute or so later. The sound was almost as irritating as the constant ringing, so I wrapped the telephone in an old blanket and put it in a big pot with the lid on. You could still hear it a little, but at least we got to eat dinner in peace and quiet.

After dinner, Mom wanted to talk about the night visitors.

"Don't worry about it," McCloud said, "I'll take care of it." He had a plan but he wouldn't tell us what it was. "Walls have ears," he said.

A few days later, Mom went to a defense committee meeting and McCloud left the house too, telling Aunt C and me not to worry. He told us to do the same things we did the night the "visitors" came. We played a little Scrabble. We turned out the lights early and checked the doors and windows before we went upstairs. Aunt C joined me, and we sat at the head of the stairs; and, just in case, she had the heavy cat-shaped doorstop and I held tight to the baseball bat.

It wasn't long before the voices began calling Aunt C's name. They called out several times. Then there was a loud thunk and a clatter like cans being thrown.

"Goddammit! Run for it!" Someone yelled.

Aunt C and I hurried down the stairs to look out the bedroom window. We got there just in time to see several figures dashing to a car running its engine. McCloud was hurling garbage at the retreating figures. As the car took off, the tires squealed on the pavement and it sped away.

When McCloud joined us, he had a big smile spread across his face.

"You look awfully pleased with yourself," Aunt C told him.

"Got license plate numbers," he said triumphantly.

"What good is that?" I asked. "The cops aren't going to help."

"I have friends," he said importantly. "There's a certain very good-looking redhead I know who works for Motor Vehicles."

"Aha," Aunt C said, "I knew it would be a woman."

"Can't help it if I'm irresistible," he grinned.

Aunt C laughed for the first time in a very long time.

A few weeks after McCloud threw garbage on the night of the visitors, the defense committee said they got reports that the harassments and the crank phone calls had stopped. We learned years later that McCloud had made a few night visits of his own along with some of his friends from the sawmill and a couple of loggers. Once the night visitors were identified, they gave up.

McCloud said it had been the work of a Catholic youth organization, followers of Father Coughlin. He said Father Coughlin was a rabid anti-unionist, anti-Communist, anti-Semite. I thought it was so weird that Catholic nuns marched for an end to the Korean War and wrote letters asking for clemency for the Rosenbergs, while Father Coughlin sold blacklists to employers to break unions, and preached hate. The whole world seemed split in two.

Chapter Eighteen

After the subpoenas, harassing phone calls, and night visits, we were going to hit back. Red and I were on our way to a demonstration protesting The Committee's hearings.

Lawyers told McCloud and Mom it wasn't a good idea for them to be there; it might mess everything up if they got arrested. Aunt C wanted to go, but the rest of us talked her out of it. She was still crying a lot and tears came to her eyes every time someone mentioned Uncle Victor.

Some people thought there might be trouble. At first, Mom wasn't going to let me go, but I begged. She relented when I promised to leave at the first sign of trouble. She said it was hard to get a teenager out of jail, and I knew she was worried I might get hurt.

⚖ ⚖ ⚖

When we were about a half-block away from the hotel where the demonstration was being held, we heard chanting. The members of The Committee were staying at the fanciest place in Seattle, the Olympic Hotel.

"Here, hold this, will you?" I said, handing my purse to my childhood friend, Red. I got a chance to see him a lot in the summer. He wouldn't be going back to college until the fall.

It was warm and I wanted to take off my jacket. "What the heck you got in this?" he asked, holding my shoulder bag by the straps. "It weighs a ton."

"Stuff I need."

"This much stuff?"

"Always be prepared!"

"You weren't a girl scout," he said accusingly.

I did carry a lot of stuff. A hair brush and comb, and lots of lipsticks; and a scarf if it rained. But it was extra heavy because I had four books I planned on returning to the library so I wouldn't get an over-due fine. Guess I didn't think it through because it was a lot to carry.

The front of the hotel was marble and gold. It gleamed in the sun like a European castle I'd seen in the movies. The picketers walked in a circle outside the entrance, chanting, "Joe, Joe, Joe must go! End the witch hunts now!"

Red and I slipped into line with the rest of the marchers. Many people nodded, telling me how sorry they were about Uncle Victor's death.

It wasn't long before several police cars arrived. They came up fast, jammed on their brakes and skidded to a stop. Doors flew open and cops jumped out. One of them, older than the rest, had gold braid on his shoulders.

I wasn't sure what to expect. I looked at Red. He seemed nervous, too.

The cop with gold braid demanded to know who was in charge. A young woman with large freckles on her face told him she was the picket captain. She didn't look much older than me. After they talked, she said we needed to move the picket line down the block, away from the entrance of the hotel.

Once the line moved back, the girl with the freckles spoke over a bullhorn. "My name is Camilla Pearl. I want to tell you what kind of people are on The Committee. One of the men is from Washington State, a Senator Canwell. He was one of the originators of the rules for the House Un-American Activities Committee."

Her hair billowed in the breeze; her voice echoed off the buildings. "This is a statement Canwell made to a reporter. The reporter asked him how Communists were identified. This was how he answered, and this is a quote: If a person says that in this country Negroes are discriminated against and that there is inequality of wealth, there is every reason to believe that person is a Communist."

The crowd broke into laughter. Then they booed.

She continued, "And who are the witnesses The Committee has called to prove their allegations? A man from the Lumberman's Association, a mill owner, a maritime employer, and two members of the Seattle Red Squad. There is also a professional witness traveling the country to every hearing!"

It was neat that a young person like her could give a speech. I was listening and at the same time looking around to see if there was something going on I might have missed when I noticed a small group of men on the edge of the demonstration. The acted like they were drunk. Somehow they didn't look like drunks - not like the old guys that hung around Pike Place Market. These men were young and healthy looking.

I grabbed Red's arm. "Something's not right," I told him.

The men staggered toward the picket line, shouting, "Commie bastards! Go back to Russia!" They kept yelling until most of the demonstrators looked at them.

Out of the corner of my eye, I saw a man pushing his way toward the young woman picket captain, who was still speaking over the bullhorn. The man wore a black watch cap, and had something in his hand. He raised his arm to hit the young woman. I swung my purse at his arm. I missed, but I got him square in the face. He fell to his knees, screeching, "My nose, my nose." Blood ran down his face.

After I hit him, a metal object dropped near him. I recognized it as a wrist pin, a car part. Uncle Victor had taught me about the different car parts when he worked on the Willys.

When the man struggled to get up, one of the demonstrators shoved him back down. He saw the wrist pin, too, and kicked it away from the man who was going to hit the girl.

"You kids, get lost!" he told us. "The cops are coming."

"Let's beat it, Joz," Red said. He grabbed me and pulled me through the crowd. He held my hand until we got across the street, away from the demonstration. We looked back to find everyone fighting. The men who pretended to be drunk were fighting alongside the police. For a second, there were bottles, rocks and someone's shoe flying through the air.

"Come on," Red said, "let's scram."

Before we could move, a black and white police car screeched to the curb in front of us. Several cops jumped out.

"You," a pink-faced cop squealed. He grabbed Red by the shoulders with hands as big as hams and he stuffed Red into the back of the police car. Off they sped. I stood with my mouth open, not believing Red had been arrested.

"Come with me," a familiar voice said.

I was relieved to see the professor.

"Joe, am I glad to see you."

I knew him because I volunteered at the Civil Rights Congress office. Even though Joe was a professor, he worked there because he had been blacklisted after the first Committee hearings in 1946. He was some kind of authority on Elizabethan literature, but he couldn't get a job. He told me he sent out over 1200 resumes. He didn't get a single reply.

Joe was bent over, like a person who spends all their time reading and writing. He was a little lame and carried a cane tipped with silver. Lame or not, he hurried me along until we got to a café and ducked inside.

"They took my friend," I blurted out. I felt like crying.

"I know, my dear."

My legs shook and my stomach knotted. We sat in a booth at the back of the café. I couldn't get the sight of Red's arrest out of my head, like a movie that kept replaying.

"I feel terrible. I hit that man. It was my fault the coppers got Red."

"I saw what you did. You were very brave."

"I don't feel brave; I feel sick."

"That's adrenalin," Joe said.

"What will happen to Red?"

"Don't worry; the defense committee will get him out. Unfortunately, they're getting experienced at that."

⚖ ⚖ ⚖

It took several days to bail Red out of jail. He came right over to see me as soon as he was released. He had a lot of bruises on his body where the cops had hit him with a billy club.

"I bet that hurt a lot," I said.

"Not at the time. Now I'm sore as hell."

"The demonstration was scary, but I'd go again."

"Me, too."

Red seemed proud of himself. He even looked older, and the mustache I had kidded him about at the concert, had grown from peach fuzz to Groucho Marx.

"Joz, let's go outside in the sun." We got two glasses of cold lemonade and walked through the breezeway to the back yard. We sat in Adirondack chairs that had been painted red. I told him about the night visitors and how McCloud had run the crumbs off.

We talked about the demonstration. It seemed like we couldn't talk about anything else. Finally, when we couldn't talk about it anymore, Red asked me something I didn't expect.

"Josie, are you worried about what people are saying - that Victor's death was a suicide?"

"More and more people are saying he committed suicide." I couldn't help it, tears came to my eyes.

"That's what articles in the newspapers say."

"Progressives should know better than to believe newspapers."

"It always seems official, when the papers say it," Red said.

I hadn't mentioned this to anyone, barely to myself, but something was gnawing at me. "Red, what if he did commit suicide?"

"What are you saying, Joz?"

"He was my hero. He was the smartest, bravest person I knew. If he killed himself, that would change everything, wouldn't it? I mean, if he wasn't the man I thought he was, maybe the things he believed in weren't right either...."

"You don't think it was suicide, do you?"

"I have to know the truth."

The tears came harder. "I can't find out anything, Red. Mom and Mc-Cloud are busy getting ready for the hearings. Goldie's still in San Francisco doing union stuff. And Aunt C? Forget it. Doctor Harmon? He won't tell us anything, or get the report for us. I don't know what to do."

"I have an idea," Red said, "there's someone who can help."

"For heaven's sake, tell me who."

"We can meet him tonight, if you're game."

"Of course I am, but I have to let Mom know where I'm going."

"I can't tell you where. You'll know why when we get there. Can you square it with your ma?

I didn't hesitate; nothing was going to keep me from the truth.

"It'll take a couple hours, tops. Meet me at Third and Pike, exactly at eight p.m., by Zales Diamond Store." He gulped his lemonade. "Gotta go, lots of things to do. Oh yeah, wear high heels, will ya? And try to look twenty-one."

He disappeared down the breezeway. I tried to guess what he was planning. Red was a pretty down-to-earth guy, married to books and school - but this was different. This was a side of him I hadn't seen. I sat in the sun for a few more minutes before I headed to the house to find clothes that would make me look older, and come up with a story for Mom of where I was going. It was one thing to go to a dance on a weeknight, but I suspected our destination was somewhere she really wouldn't approve.

Chapter Nineteen

When I got to Third and Pike, Red was leaning against the window of Zale's Diamond Store. Neon lights blinked messages: Brilliant Values, Easy Credit, We help couples say "I love you." I thought about the mines in South Africa and vowed never to wear a diamond ring. Somehow visions of diamond miners living under apartheid was not a romantic picture.

Red let out a whistle. "Hey doll, you got the time?"

I sang a bit of Lefty Frizzle's *Honky Tonkn'*. "If you got the money, I got the time - we'll go honky tonkn' and we'll have a time...."

"You look neat, Joz."

"You're looking pretty snazzy yourself."

He was wearing a gray porkpie hat with a tiny red feather tucked in the hat band.

"What's this?" I inspected the bowl of a pipe peeping out of his jacket pocket.

"A Meerschaum," he said, "My grandfather's."

"Are you really going to smoke that thing?"

"How do I look?" He put the pipe between his lips and posed, showing his profile.

"You look like a college student. Oh, that's right, you are a college student."

"You look real neat, Josie."

"My feet are killing me." Aunt C's fire engine red stiletto heels weren't made for human feet.

"You've got your hair up."

He told me to try to look older, so I did my hair up in a French roll, borrowed a pair of outlandishly big red earrings from Mom, one of Aunt C's black silk blouses and dressy jacket.

"Let's bust outta here," he said. A bus bound for the University District pulled up. Most of the passengers were sitting at the front of the bus. We had the back seat to ourselves. This was the choice seat for young people where they could spread out and talk loud.

"Okay, what's the big mystery, where are we going?" I asked.

"The Blue Moon."

"Where all those bohemians hang out? I was afraid of this."

"Can't be all bad, the professor goes there," Red argued.

"We're meeting the professor?"

He nodded. "When he bailed me out of the can he said he had information about Victor's death, and Dr. Harmon."

"But I see the professor at the Civil Rights office," I protested. "Why should we go to the Blue Moon?"

"You know the office is bugged. I thought you were in a hurry to get info about your uncle's death."

"Mom is gonna kill me for this...." I knew Mom wouldn't want me to go someplace where they serve booze, but I was dying to find out what information the professor had.

⚖ ⚖ ⚖

The bus route we took was a four lane stretch going both ways, a total of eight lanes of traffic. After we rumbled across the University Bridge, we were on the outskirts of the U-district. Even across a full eight lanes of traffic, the sign over the Blue Moon stood out like a beacon. We got off and made our way across the wide streets to the doorway under the brightly lit sign with a woman reclining on a blue crescent moon.

We hesitated, standing at the open doorway in a blue glow from the neon sign.

"I'm not so sure this is a good idea," I said.

There was music coming from the tavern. The band was playing *You Belong to Me.*

"Ready?" Red asked.

"Not really," *God, I hope no one realizes I'm not of age.* "Okay, let's go."

He pushed the porkpie hat further back on his head, took my arm, and we stepped into a smoke filled room. The blue haze made everything look fuzzy, almost magical. Small neon beer signs blinked off and on, reminding me of lights at Christmas.

Red pointed to an empty booth near the door. I teetered after him, hoping the high heels weren't making me look like a dope. Once we were seated a waitress appeared. She chomped a wad of gum like a cow chewing a cud. She looked me up and down. *Is she gonna kick me out? She must know I'm not 21.*

"What kinda beer you kids want?"

"Two bottles of Green Death," Red told her.

"Rainier Ale it is," she said and trotted off to get our order.

"Green Death?" I asked.

"That's what the guys at college drink," he explained. "Rainier Brewery is the oldest brewery around; once it was the biggest one west of the Mississippi. But I'd rather drink it than talk about it," he added.

"Seems you know an awful lot about beer and taverns."

"A bunch of us started going to a tavern near the college," he explained. "No one checks our ages. We have a few beers, talk and listen to music."

⚖ ⚖ ⚖

While we waited for the waitress to bring the Green Death, we looked around, sizing up the place.

"Joz, see that guy leaning against the bar?" Red pointed to a man wearing a Hawaiian shirt. He had muscles bulging from his upper arms. "That's Freddie Steele. Once he was the world middleweight boxing champ. Now he's a bouncer!"

"I'll try to behave myself," I promised.

In a far corner, the jazz combo played *Summertime*. An older Negro man with graying hair was at the piano; a drummer and horn player accompanied him.

"The guy at the piano, Mr. Know-It-All, that's Oscar Holden," I said. "He played with Count Basie and the drummer is Ted Wooten."

"How do you know that?"

"You aren't the only one that gets around."

Of course I didn't get around. Mr. Holden was the father of a kid from Garfield who lived down the street, and the drummer happened to be a friend of Uncle Victor and Aunt Celeste's. Seattle was a small town.

The waitress returned with two glasses and two bottles of beer. "Here's yer vitamin R," she said. The label on the beer was bright green with a big letter R in the center for the Rainier Brewing Company.

Red asked her if the professor was there. "He's in the back, hon. Want me to get him for you?"

"Over there," I pointed and waved at the professor.

He was sitting at a table with some men and women who were all talking and laughing all at once. When he saw us, he made his way over to our booth.

"Good evening Madam," he said, bowing to me.

My, my, aren't we formal.

The professor leaned against his silver-tipped cane. He turned to Red. "Here's stuff indeed to shame us all. Pray, whose advice did you take in this learned letter?"

What the heck is the professor talking about? Letter? What letter? And why is he speaking like that…sounds like he's on stage…

"The Black Prince, sir, alias the prince of darkness, alias the Devil."

Even more strange was Red's answer.

"I take thy word," the professor continued, "and with that thee for mine; come then, let's more confer of this anon."

The professor motioned for us to follow him. When I tried to go with them my feet told me no. "In a sec," I told Red. My toes and heels were killing me and I thought if I kicked my shoes off the throbbing might stop.

They went to a table where the professor's friends gathered. They laughed, and said odd things like the professor had done.

There was a full glass of beer in front of me. I didn't want to call attention to myself for not being 21, but I didn't want to drink it. I had made a promise to Mom I wouldn't drink outside our house. In our family, there were special occasions when we had beer at supper - hot summer evenings when our meal was potato salad, dried herring and cold cuts. There was a glass bowl on the table with an unlit candle in it. I looked around and no one was looking at me so I poured half the Green Death into the glass bowl with the candle and pushed it aside.

I amused myself by people-watching; there was a couple slow-dancing as the band played *We Belong Together*. They were so close you couldn't get a cigarette paper between them. The tavern was half full of people. The professor and his friends took up two long tables at the rear of the room opposite the band. Small tables and chairs were scattered around the room, where couples sat whispering and looking at each other with calf eyes. At the long wooden bar a Negro in Army uniform played dice with the bartender. There were several interracial couples, something you saw in the Central District, but not usually in places like the University District.

This was the first time I had ever been in a tavern. I was so caught up watching everything I hadn't noticed when he slid into the seat across from me. It was magic, one of those once in a lifetime events, something you read about in a dime novel - the handsome stranger appears from nowhere. And he was the most!

"Can I buy you a beer?" he asked. He was older, maybe thirty-something with dark hair and dark eyebrows. He was so good-looking I swallowed before I found words to answer.

"No, thank you," I mumbled.

"Jack, come on - they're all waiting," a slightly balding man puffing on a pipe urged him to leave.

"Kinda busy here, Larry," Jack told him.

"Busy with monkey business," the bald one answered.

"You look lonesome," Jack said, "Why don't you join us?" He motioned to where Red and the professor were sitting. "You have a terrific face," he said, "fantastic cheekbones."

"I'm waiting for someone," I stammered. But my feet were still killing me, and I couldn't have gone with him even if I wanted.

"Ja-ack," his friend insisted.

"If you change your mind, you know where to find ...." He flashed a smile that melted me down to the bottom of my toes.

"They're waiting," Larry prodded.

Jack slid out of the booth and followed his friend to the table in the rear of the room. He turned back to give me a wink and a nod. "Later, gorgeous."

His voice was like a song in my head: Terrific face - fantastic cheekbones! Gorgeous! So what if he was an older guy?

There was a commotion when Jack and his friend sat down at the professor's table. Everyone talked at once, shook hands, slapped shoulders and hugged.

⚖ ⚖ ⚖

The waitress appeared and put another bottle of Green Death on the table in front of me.

"What's this?" I asked, "I didn't order anything."

"From the cutie pie, "she replied, "Who was that?"

"All I know is his name was Jack."

"Yum," she answered.

The band played *Hurry On Down*. Every once in a while a woman's shrill laugh sounded above the music and I heard snatches of conversations" - Dave Beck, biggest labor sellout in the country...."

"Bullshit!"

"Joe Louis was the best...."

"Hubba, hubba."

The band began playing a strange tune with lots of horn and drumming. As the music grew louder, a warm pulsing began in my chest, spread through my body to every nerve. My heart was beating with the drums. There was no talking, no laughter, everyone in the room was part of the music, one giant throbbing wave. Then it stopped. The whole room exploded cheering the band.

⚖ ⚖ ⚖

When Red joined me he was in a hurry to leave. "We gotta get outta here, Joz."

"What's happening?"

"There's an undercover cop here, we gotta hightail it."

"But...."

"Josie, please, I'm out on bail, I don't wanna go back to the can!"

It had been hard for the defense committee to raise money to bail Red out after he got arrested at the demonstration. I didn't want him to get arrested again. I forced my swollen feet back into Aunt C's stiletto heels and hobbled to the door. The professor waited for us at the exit.

He still talked in that strange way. "Revenge shall sweeten what my grief's have tasted," he said, raising a schooner of beer in salute. "Remember, sir, what you have to do; be wise and resolute." He made a slight bow and melted into the crowd. Red took my arm and we stepped outside into the cool night air.

Chapter Twenty

It was good to be away from the smell of stale beer and cigarettes. I inhaled the fresh air like a thirsty man gulps water. We heard the band playing a strange tune as we waited for the bus. It sounded off-key to me. My attention to the music was interrupted when a man started yelling.

"Hey, you two. Stop!"

"I bet that's the cop," Red said. "He musta gone out the back door and down the alley."

At times, you're unbelievably lucky, because the bus's arrival couldn't have been more perfect. It roared up and we jumped on. The driver slammed the doors shut. "Hang on," he said, gunning the motor across the intersection before the light turned red. "I'm already late," he explained, giving the bus even more gas.

We looked out the back window and saw the man who had yelled at us shaking his fist in the air.

Again, we had the back seat and spread out on the choice spot. "Rats, I hate these things," I said, removing Aunt C's killer shoes. I rubbed my sore feet. "Boy, this night was a bust." *You have fantastic cheekbones....* "On second thought, maybe not a complete bust."

"It wasn't a bust," Red smiled. "For you, from the professor." He handed me a folded piece of paper.

The handwritten note read: *J. Doctor Harmon claims he found a suicide note. He says he destroyed it to protect Victor's reputation, yet he is talking to many people about it. It is now an open secret. It appears the doctor is working to discredit your uncle. J.B.*

"That rat doctor. He's been lying all the time!"

"Don't get upset, Joz, maybe this note can help."

I wasn't sure what I would do, but one thing for sure, Dr. Harmon was going to have to answer for his lies. I hoped the note would motivate Mom and Aunt C to work harder for answers about Uncle Victor's death.

⚖ ⚖ ⚖

We were almost at our transfer point when I remembered the shenanigans Red went through with the professor. "What was all that stuff you and the professor were talking? I felt like I woke up in the middle of a play."

"It was from a play," he laughed. "A play by John Ford, *Tis A Pity She's a Whore,* second act. Gee, Joz, I thought you knew about the game."

"How would I know about some college stuff?"

"Sorry, I thought everyone knew." He explained that the professor and some of his ex-students play for beers. The first person who talks and doesn't quote a line of Old English literature has to pay for the beer. They say the professor always wins.

⚖ ⚖ ⚖

When we got home, I insisted Red crap out on the couch. I wanted him to be there in the morning when I owned up to Mom about going to the Blue Moon.

I told Red, "That guy Jack offered to buy me a beer. He was kinda cute. I hadn't forgotten about Alain, but that Jack guy really was cute...."

"He's some writer from Frisco," Red said. "He wrote some book called *The Town and the City*. That Italian cat with him writes poetry and publishes stuff. They came to hang out with the professor and the writers from the UW. They were all mad about the prof getting fired."

"I had fun people-watching," I told him. "It was kind of exciting. I liked listening to Mr. Holden on the piano. Except that last piece they were doing when we left sounded off key."

"Everyone was talking about that piece, before they played it. It's experimental - a work in progress," Red explained. "And get this: it's called *Goodbye to the Porkpie Hat!*"

We couldn't quit laughing. He picked up his Porkpie hat, put it on my head and pulled it down over my eyes.

"Goodbye," he said.

"And goodnight," I said.

I gave Red blankets and a pillow for the couch and headed upstairs to my room. There was so much to think about - Alain, the real live French sailor, or the dark haired stranger with the sexy voice.

"Josie, wait!" Red called out, stopping me half way up the stairs. "About tonight, did you feel you learned anything? Anything that might help get to the truth about Victor's death?"

In all the excitement, I had forgotten about the professor's note.

"I mean, you were pretty upset you weren't getting any answers," Red reminded me.

"I feel better," I said. "Maybe Aunt C will stop seeing that quack doctor when she reads the professor's note."

"If I can help, you'll let me know?"

"You can help. Be with me when I talk to Mom tomorrow."

"Jeez, Joz, that's scarier than going to jail." He laughed when he said it, but it had a ring of truth. Mom could get pretty angry sometimes.

By the time I crawled under the covers, I had forgotten all about Jack and wondered how my friend Red had gotten so grown-up and wise. Everybody was changing.

Chapter Twenty-One

I had been up for hours, and Red was still snoring on the couch, Hemingway's *The Old Man and the Sea* on his chest.

"Red, get up. I'm not taking the rap by myself." I poked him and he grunted.

Mom was at the kitchen table surrounded by papers, typing on the Selectric typewriter. The union had purchased the electric typewriter for Uncle Victor because he wrote a lot of reports and articles for their newspaper. I loved it because there was a typing class at school with the same machine and it gave me a chance to practice at home.

"What are you working on?" I asked Mom.

"Minutes for the defense committee."

There was a mass of papers and notes on the table. I cleared a spot and poured a cup of coffee for Red and a glass of milk for me.

"What's up?" Mom said, looking at the two of us. "You look like the proverbial cat that swallowed the canary."

"I have a confession," I began.

"Something happen at the Madison Y dance?"

"Uh, we didn't exactly go to the Y."

She stared, waiting for an explanation.

"My fault," Red volunteered. "It was my idea."

"Still waiting," Mom said. I felt her eyes boring a hole in me.

I reminded her how I had said my friend Jennie Boggs was going to the Y dance. "I didn't really say I was going with her."

Her eyes got darker.

Once more, Red jumped in. "She didn't know where we were going."

She shifted her gaze to him.

"We went to the Blue Moon," I said.

"What on earth for?"

I explained how I felt so bad. "We weren't getting any information about the cause of Uncle Victor's death. There were so many rumors and gossip. When Red told me he might know someone who had information, I jumped at the chance. That's why we went to the Blue Moon, to see the professor. I won't lie, Mom; I wanted to go. I was sick of waiting for answers."

I showed her the note from the professor. "Doctor Harmon is telling people he found a suicide note from Uncle Victor."

"A suicide note? There was no note!" Mom said. "Goldie and I were here before the doc came. We would have found it, if there was one."

"Show the note to Aunt C, Mom."

"I'll try, but I don't think it'll make any difference. She worships Doctor Harmon."

"But it looks like he's working with the Feds," I argued.

"If he started the rumor there was a suicide note," she agreed.

"Do you think what the professor wrote might convince Aunt C?"

She shook her head.

"Then what we did is useless."

"It wasn't useless," Mom pointed out. "We know we're on the right track. We have to get to the truth out of Harmon."

Red stared into his coffee cup. "I'm sorry, really, sorry I tricked Josie into going to the Blue Moon."

"Look," Mom said, "I admire that you had the imagination to do something. Even doing something you might get into trouble for. But I don't want Josie to hang around a place like that. For that matter Red, you aren't twenty-one yet, are you?"

"Nineteen. Last month."

"You shouldn't be going there, either."

What's wrong with the Blue Moon?" I asked.

"A lot of well-known people go there," Red argued. "Guys from Frisco were there last night. Some hotshot writer and a poet."

"I know all about the Blue Moon," Mom said. "I know what those places are like."

"I thought it was pretty cool." Red smiled.

"Oh, really cool, all right," Mom said. "That's the problem. Josie, didn't you say some guy offered to buy you a beer, and asked you to join him?"

"Yeah, Jack. Everybody in the place was making over him like he was some celebrity."

"How old was this character?" she asked.

"Kinda old, like McCloud and Aunt C..."

"My age, you mean?"

I nodded.

"You think it's okay for an older guy to buy beer and try to get to know a young woman half his age?"

"It was kinda strange," I admitted.

Red broke in, "But why shouldn't I hang out there? I mean when I'm legal age."

"I guess it depends on what you want to do with your life."

"But, Mom, Aunt C knows all those artists and they're a cool crowd."

"Ask yourself, who did she marry? Uncle Victor, the most down-to-earth guy. Someone she could count on. There are lots of iffy things that go on at the Blue Moon and with the artsy crowd, but Celeste chooses not to be part of that. Too many people get hurt. It's only the art with her. If someone wants a foot-loose life, that's okay. In your case, Josie, you aren't old enough to make that choice. I'm not sure you are, either," she told Red.

⚖ ⚖ ⚖

She didn't punish me; she asked me to promise I wouldn't do anything like it again, and she said she would talk to Aunt C about the professor's note. I hoped Aunt C would finally see that Doctor Harmon was not on the up-and-up.

That night Mom kept her word about speaking with Aunt C. They were in Aunt C's bedroom and you could hear them all over the house; not so much Mom, but Aunt C.

Aunt C was loud. "I don't care who says what, not even the professor. I don't know what I'd do without Dr. Harmon."

Mom was talking, but I couldn't make out what she said. I sat in the living room with McCloud; we pretended we couldn't hear the conversation in the bedroom.

"Leave me alone," Aunt C yelled.

"I want my sister back!" Mom yelled.

McCloud ducked his head into the Seattle Star as Mom stormed out of Aunt C's room, shaking her head. "I'm gonna throttle her," she said, her voice quavering. She went into the kitchen, the double doors banging after her.

McCloud shook his head sadly.

"Can't we do something?" I asked.

"If I knew what to do, kiddo, I would." He turned back to his newspaper and Mom banged pots and pans in the kitchen.

An idea popped into my head. Later, I went to the kitchen to help Mom who was chopping carrots like she was lopping off someone's head with each smack of the knife. I stayed out of her way, all the while thinking about what I could do to change things.

⚖ ⚖ ⚖

The next day, I decided to go to Harmon's office. I had the professor's note in my pocket and I kept touching it like it was a rabbit's foot.

I memorized the note: *J. Doctor Harmon claims he found a suicide note. He says he destroyed it to protect Victor's reputation, yet he is talking to many people about it. It is now an open secret. It appears the doctor is working to discredit your uncle. Signed, J.B.*

I got downtown just before it was time to start work, and was surprised how many people were in the lobby of the medical building. The place was jammed with men in suits, secretaries with beauty shop "do's" and nurses all in white, from the tip of their toes to the top of their starched white hats. An elevator operator attendant dressed in dark purple was directing traffic to the elevators. He pointed with white gloved hands and clicked a black clicker to let the operators know they should shut the doors and start their ascent.

It was exciting trying to negotiate the crowd and get on the right elevator. Many were express and I looked for one that would let me off on a lower floor.

When I got out of the elevator the hallway was deserted and my footsteps sounded like I was in a cave, only one made of marble, glass and polished wood. Harmon's waiting room was half-full of people. The nurse wearing the lime-colored sweater appeared and told me to have a seat. She announced that the doctor had been delayed at Harborview, the county hospital.

An old woman wearing a hat with a yellow flower told me, "I bet it's because of the epidemic."

"What epidemic?" I asked.

"Polio," she said almost in a whisper, "Infantile Paralysis." I noticed several people shudder when she said it.

The nurse peered into the room, and I jumped up before she went back to the area with the exam rooms.

"I have an emergency," I said, and brushed past her.

I found the doctor in his office, looking out the window with his hands clasped behind his back. "I have to speak to you," I announced.

"I'm sorry, Doctor," the nurse told him. "She jumped ahead of others. I wanted you to have a second to drink your coffee and catch your breath before seeing patients."

"Don't I know you?" he asked, seating himself at his desk. He took a sip of coffee from a paper cup.

"Josie Thompson, Celeste and Victor Jenkins' niece."

"Ahh," he said. "I remember, you weren't very pleased with me."

Dr. Harmon looked clean and crisp in a freshly ironed shirt, but his eyes drooped like he hadn't slept.

"Here!" I threw the professor's note on the desk.

He opened the folded paper and read it, looking at it for a long time. "It's an opinion," he said.

"Did you say you found a suicide note from my uncle?"

"No," he said, trying to stare me down.

"You're supposed to help people!" I yelled. "The professor didn't make this up."

He sighed. "If there's nothing else, I have patients. He folded the paper and handed it back to me. I grabbed it and put it in my pocket.

"Didn't you take an oath to do no harm?"

Just for a second, a look crossed his face that had guilt written all over it. He walked quickly to the door. "It's time for you to leave, young lady."

I dashed out of his office and left through his private exit. Just before the door closed I yelled, "Liar! Liar!" The private door closed and locked behind me. By the time I reached the elevators, I was crying.

What was I thinking? Of course he wasn't going to confess - this was so stupid.

An elevator made its way up the shaft. I felt cold air that made me shiver. Tears filled my eyes making everything a blur. My face was buried in a handkerchief when two men got off the elevator. Out of the corner of my eye I noticed that both men, dressed in suits, looked familiar. They went straight to Harmon's private door.

"Getting on, Miss?" the elevator operator asked.

I shook my head, putting the handkerchief in front of my face as I watched one of the men unlock Harmon's private door. I was sure one of them was Agent Brock. I raced to the door as it started to close behind them just before it snapped shut. Slowly I opened the door and listened.

"Ahh, Doctor Harmon."

I recognized Brock's voice.

"How did you get in here?" Harmon demanded.

"We have our ways," Brock answered.

"How did you know I was here? This is usually my day off."

"Yer fancy car, the Rocket 88 in the parking lot. Can't miss it, it's as big as a B-17 bomber.

"Get out of my office."

Slowly, I opened the door wider and stepped into the hallway.

"Look, doc, we got a problem," Brock said.

"More threats?" the doctor asked.

"We have another little job for you," Brock's partner said. He spoke with a southern drawl.

"I don't have time for this," Harmon told him.

"Take a look at this," the agent with the drawl said.

"Where did you get this? This is a patient's chart. This is a breach of confidentiality!"

"Don't be a horse's ass," Brock sneered. "You've done worse."

"Much worse!" the other agent added.

"There was a long silence. Then the doctor said," I did what you asked. Now get the hell out."

"Doc, is that any way to act?" Brock asked.

"No more! The business with the so-called suicide note from Jenkins was one thing; but this - I won't drug a patient. I won't do it!"

"The hell you won't," Brock told Harmon. "Unless you want to be a guest on McNeil Island, you'll cooperate. And I mean a long-term guest. All I have to do is drop a dime. Got the phone number right here, Washington State Insurance Commission. One dime, that's all...."

"It's not nice to falsify medical claims," the other agent drawled. "Seems our good doctor here had a lapse in judgment. Of course we understand."

"Shame about your son," Brock said, "but the law is the law."

"Don't speak about my son."

"Hate to be in your shoes, doc," the other agent drawled. "Lovely wife, a kid with Cerebral Palsy - what are people gonna say when they end up on welfare? And you're in the pen for defrauding an insurance company?"

I made my way to Doctor Harmon's office and stood in the open doorway.

"Just do what yer told, doc," Brock's partner shoved a bottle of pills at him.

The two agents were standing with their backs to me. Harmon looked up. He was startled when he saw me. The agents noticed and turned.

"Cat's out of the bag!" I said.

"Listen, kid," Brock said starting toward me.

I didn't hear the rest of it. I took off fast, dashing into the hallway and heading toward the stairs. There were footsteps behind me as I raced down the stairs, taking two and three steps at a time. When I reached the lobby, the door banged shut behind me. It was easy to melt into the crowd of people waiting for the elevator.

I kept my eyes on the stairway door, trying to catch my breath. There was no sign of the agents. Finally, when my heart stopped trying to leap out of my chest, the two Feds emerged from an elevator. I zigzagged through the crowd and bolted into the street. My mind was racing, trying to figure out my next move when a voice stopped me.

"Hey good-lookin', where you headed?" McCloud leaned against a light pole smoking a cigarette.

"McCloud!"

"Glad to see me?" He touched two fingers to his temple saluting someone behind me. I turned to find Brock and his partner a few feet away.

"Your chariot awaits," McCloud said, as his maroon 1950 Ford pulled up to the curb. Red was driving. McCloud opened the front door of the car with a flourish and I dove into the safety of the front seat.

"Don't take any wooden nickels," he said to the agents as he climbed into the back seat and slammed the door.

"I didn't know you could drive," I said to Red.

"Maiden voyage," Red replied, hitting the gas pedal. The car lurched down the street in low gear.

"How did you know I'd be here?"

"Your pal," he motioned to Red.

"I know you, Josie," Red said. "I knew you wouldn't leave it alone after we got the professor's note. I had a hunch there'd be trouble."

"If you hadn't come out in the next few seconds, I was gonna go in and tear Harmon's office apart if I had to," McCloud added.

The car lurched forward again and Red hit the brakes hard.

"Concentrate on driving," McCloud told him. "Give her a little gas, push the clutch in, shift into second like I showed you and let the clutch out slowly. Slowly!"

On the way, I felt in my pocket to see if the professor's note was still there. It had seemed like a good omen and it was. Now we knew why Harmon acted the way he did. It was no longer a guess that the Feds had something on him. To me, it was almost proof Uncle Victor didn't commit suicide. But we still didn't know how he died.

"Josie, what's the skinny?" McCloud asked.

"Plenty, we got the low-down now!" I told him and Red everything I overheard the agents say to Harmon.

"Now, the big question," McCloud said, "if it wasn't suicide then what?"

"That's what I've been thinking," I told him.

"It means it's even more important we get that coroner's report," Red commented.

⚖ ⚖ ⚖

When we got home, we found a message on the refrigerator from Mom to McCloud. It said: There's mail for you on the table by the door. You're going to love it!

McCloud opened the envelope. The return address was the U.S. Government Printing Office. Inside was a small blue booklet entitled Rules of Procedure, Committee on Un-American Activities.

"Listen to this," McCloud read from the booklet. "Public Law 601, 79th Congress - blah, blah, blah. The committee - is authorized to make investigations - of un-American propaganda, activities in the United States - diffusion of subversive and un-American - propaganda - and attacks the principle of the form of government as guaranteed by our Constitution."

"So much for freedom of speech," McCloud snickered.

"Oh, listen to this one, "...any witness desiring to make a prepared or written statement - shall file a copy - in advance - All such statements, upon approval by The Committee may be inserted in the official transcript."

"This is the one I love," Red said, reading over his shoulder. "Counsel will not be permitted to engage in oral argument with The committee - but shall confine his activity to the area of legal advice - failure to do so shall - subject counsel to disciplinary action which may include warning, censure, removing from the hearing room of counsel, or a recommendation of contempt proceedings."

"Remember, the professor's lawyer got a contempt charge," Red said. "After that it was hard for anyone subpoenaed to even find a lawyer around Seattle to represent them. The few that would were so busy that's almost all they did."

"Think I'll keep my copy," McCloud said, "along with my comic book and baseball card collection."

⚖ ⚖ ⚖

When Mom and Aunt C got home from grocery shopping, I told them about my trip to Doctor Harmon's office.

"The Feds are blackmailing him," Mom said after I finished.

"It sounded like the doctor didn't want to do what they were asking," I said.

"The Feds will use anything they can to get the results they want, no matter how dirty," Mom commented. "What do you think, Celeste?"

Aunt C sat, just shaking her head.

I wondered what would happen to Harmon's kid if his dad was sent to prison. Before Mom got a job, we had to go to Harborview, the county hospital, when we got sick. It wasn't any fun. You only went if you were dying. There were long lines, a long wait before you were seen, and sometimes the people who worked there weren't very nice. A few years ago, it got cleaned up and they hired more doctors and nurses. It got fixed after a big scandal when someone died. I wondered what would happen to Harmon's kid if he had to use Harborview?

Aunt C listened to everything I said about my visit to Harmon's office and thanked me. Then she went to the kitchen to start supper. She didn't act upset about the news. It seemed no matter what, she wasn't going to change her mind about the doctor.

Chapter Twenty-Two

I woke up with a bad feeling. This was the big day, one I dreaded. Mom and McCloud had to appear before The Committee.

I dressed and spent a lot of time in front of the mirror trying to make my face look relaxed and not worried. There was plenty to worry about: What if Mom went to jail? McCloud could handle it; he had been in a war, had people shooting at him. But Mom? And what would happen to me and Aunt C if we were left alone?

⚖ ⚖ ⚖

When Mom, McCloud, Red and I got to the County City Building, the sidewalk was filled with people protesting the hearings. Signs called the hearings "witch hunts." Several men were snapping pictures of the demonstrators. A TV crew with bright lights recording the event caught my eye.

We made our way through the crowd to the entrance of the building. A dozen sheriffs stood at the top of the steps.

"Good luck," a man Mom knew said as we passed.

"Give 'em hell," another shouted.

"Hey, McCloud," a man dressed in work clothes shouted and waved. He wore a red plaid shirt and blue jeans. "What kinda cigarettes you smoke?" he laughed.

"Screw you, Frank," McCloud shot back. Then he laughed. "He means he'll visit me in jail and bring me smokes," he told me. McCloud was still grinning.

We made our way through the crowd to the entrance as the crowd began to chant: "Joe, Joe, Joe must go. End the witch hunts now!"

A sheriff with a huge belly stood blocking the entrance. He asked us our business. Mom and McCloud showed him their subpoenas. He motioned to two other uniformed men and each walked with Mom and McCloud into the building and disappeared down a long hallway.

I showed my pass and he opened the door. My heart was beating fast. Red followed behind. There were two more uniformed men in front of the double doors of the court room. It gave me a chill to see so many uniformed men with huge guns strapped around their waists.

"You," the sheriff motioned to Red. "That door." He pointed down the hall.

"Me?"

"Gotta press card, don't cha?"

"Oh, yeah." Red stuck the press card from the union's newspaper in the band of his porkpie hat. "Good luck," he whispered to me before heading to the door reserved for the press, radio and TV.

Mom and Aunt C had arranged for me and Red to get into the hearing room. Not an easy feat: The Committee was notorious for only letting those who agreed with them into the hearings. They didn't want a repeat of the 1948 hearings.

In '48 they had made the mistake of holding public hearings in the old armory. The room was large and huge crowds attended. There were cries of "kangaroo court" that stopped the proceedings. Old Reverend Corywicks, who performed the service to marry my aunt and uncle, was dragged out of the hearing by the police.

After the protests at the armory, The Committee held their hearings in small rooms. Only people with Committee-issued passes or press cards were allowed in. Red got a press pass from Uncle Victor's union paper, and he agreed to write a report on the hearings for them.

Mom got a pass for me from a friend of a friend who was a member of the DAR, the Daughters of the American Revolution. Admittance was refused to known radicals, so it was decided Aunt C shouldn't try. It seemed like she didn't want to go anyway, so I got the chance.

A guard opened the huge double doors to the hearing room, then blocked the entrance.

"Let's see your pass," he demanded.

I held my breath as he examined the paper carefully. He stared at me.

"Civics class," I said.

"It's summer." His eyes narrowed.

"Summer school." I gave him a big smile.

"Guess it's okay." He motioned me in.

The room filled up quickly; I guessed about a hundred people, including the press and TV. I recognized one of the newsmen from KING, Channel Five, Charles Herring from Early Edition News. He had the only live news program this side of LA. While it was exciting having TV coverage of big events and seeing them so quickly after they happened, they often twisted the news or left out important information. Would they make Mom or McCloud look like traitors or something sinister?

I was curious about who came to the hearings. There were half a dozen guys wearing VFW hats sitting together. Most of the people in the crowd were men, many of them older, in their late forties or early fifties. I had them pegged for coppers, maybe even the Red Squad. Most of the women were older, and kind of drab looking. One woman, about Mom's age, stood out. She wore a wide brimmed hat with a pheasant feather that bobbed up and down when she moved. Her coat was a green that made her bright red lipstick stand out. I wondered if she was the woman Mom knew from the DAR.

I spotted a reporter from the Cannery Workers Union, an Oriental guy who was the only person in the room who wasn't white, except for an old Negro man. The old man had gray hair and wore spectacles that slid down his nose.

People spoke in hushed voices. High ceilings made sound reverberate around the room. There was a lot of dark brown wood on the walls. The color was as dark as the sky during the storm on the day Uncle Victor died, almost black. Guards wearing guns stood at every door. An American flag hung in one corner of the room and a Washington State flag in the other. A painting of George Washington hung on the wall. Every school room and government building in the state had a picture of Old George. I guess it was always the same painting. From first grade on, I saw paintings where he wore a white powdered wig that seems to melt into the clouds behind him, some kind of angel looking down on us from up high.

Several young men wearing suits whispered, distributing papers to the eight men seated at a long table stretching the length of the front of the room. The table shone with a thousand coats of wax. Microphones were placed on the table in an eagle's nest of electric cords. The eight men were The Committee. They sat in padded leather chairs with armrests. One of them tilted back, disappearing from view behind the table.

Red sat with the reporters in an area separated from the spectators. A makeshift sign on the wall behind them read "Press Only." He got into the part, like he had at the Blue Moon when we snuck in to see the professor. He was chatting with the press people, pad in hand and pencil stuck behind his ear. He looked like a real reporter. No one would have guessed the union had given him the press pass so there would be another friendly face for Mom and McCloud.

Lights for the TV cameras lit up the courtroom, casting sharp shadows that made the place look unreal. The lights were hot, adding to the discomfort of sitting on wooden seats where the spectators sat. But most disturbing was The Committee, whispering, talking behind their hands, eyes searching the room like animals looking for prey.

⚖ ⚖ ⚖

Finally the hearing started. "Order! Order! The Committee is in session," said one of The Committee, banging his gavel. He made me think of an aging movie actor. He wore a ring with a gem so big it sparkled like Captain Marvel's lightning bolt. I was no Billy Batson, but it was clear to me who the bad guys were. If only uttering "Shazam!" would vanquish them!

A sign said the one who looked like an aging movie actor was Harold H. Velde. He always used an initial for his middle name which happened to be Himmel! Mom said it meant "heaven sent." He wasn't heaven sent, that's for sure, just the opposite.

126

"I will now turn the proceedings over to the Acting Chairman, Mr. Morgan Moulder," Velde announced.

Moulder was almost bald. He tried to cover his head with a few dark strands of hair combed from one side over the top of his head. He was a senator from Missouri. According to Mom and McCloud, his only claim to fame was hosting "The Cured Ham Breakfast" at the Speakers Dining Room in the Capitol Building. Sweat poured down Moulder's face from the hot TV lights. He constantly dabbed at his forehead with a handkerchief. He spoke in a monotone.

"This is the sub-committee of the U.S. Congress House Committee on Un-American Activities - blah, blah, blah. I wish to thank the Honorable - blah, blah, thanks to Mayor blah, blah, the Board of blah, blah, Sheriff blah, blah, members of blah, blah and their staff...."

He kept droning on and my backside was numb from the hard seat and my brain was turning to mush. Another member of The Committee leaned back in his big leather chair and disappeared from view. *Wonder if that jackass is taking a nap? Lucky duck if he is.*

Moulder continued, "I desire to announce - blah, blah, blah. On and on he went. When he finally finished I guessed what he said was that anyone making a disturbance would be thrown out of the hearing room. He had droned on so long that three of the guys wearing VFW hats were asleep and a couple of men that looked like they were from the Red Squad snored. Moulder himself appeared sleepy.

He shook himself, and said more "blah, blah." It took almost five minutes for him to say the TV crew and photographers could take pictures, except when the witnesses were talking.

Moulder was starting more "blah, blah" when Senator Velde interrupted. "I certainly want to say, Mr. Moulder, that I concur - I do feel we should protect the freedom of the press as much as possible instead of merely protecting the so - called rights of some of the witnesses who will appear here."

So-called rights of the witness?

"I will now turn the proceedings over to counsel, the honorable Mr. Tavenner," Moulder announced.

Thank goodness. Maybe we would finally get to the hearings. Mental note: *ask Mom or McCloud if they think boring you to death is part of The Committee strategy - to wear you down? Bore you to death so you would rather be in jail....*

The lawyer for The Committee, Mr. Tavenner announced, "The first witness is Camilla Pearl."

A young woman was escorted into the room by a sheriff. I recognized her as the young picket captain from the demonstration where Red had gotten arrested. I had hit the goon with my purse when he tried to hurt her.

"State your name for the record."

"Camilla Pearl."

"Do you live on the 2100 block of Ravenna Boulevard in Seattle, Washington?"

She nodded.

"You must speak, for the record," he said briskly.

He asked questions about where she went to school. Each time she refused to answer, taking the 5th Amendment.

"Let me ask you this: Are you enrolled at the University of Washington?"

"I refuse to answer on the 5th Amendment. I do not have to testify against myself!"

He shuffled papers and glared at her.

The question sounded innocent, but it wasn't. Uncle Victor had explained how it worked: If she told them where she went to school they could ask her questions about her professors, her friends, and her fellow students. If she didn't answer, she could be sent to jail for contempt of court. That was the way this outfit operated: answer what seemed an innocent question, and the next thing you knew, you had the choice of ratting on your friends or going to jail.

After they finished with the young woman, the sheriff led her out of the courtroom. We heard her muffled cries, "Let go of my arm, you fascist! You're hurting me!"

⚖ ⚖ ⚖

Moulder asked The Committee's attorney, Mr. Tavenner, to call the next witness. Tavenner called Mom. I was breathing so hard that my heart fluttered. I told myself I wouldn't be scared, but an electric feeling went through my body. My stomach hurt. I took deep breaths, the way Uncle Victor told me to do deep breathing. Finally, things quit swimming before my eyes and sounding like the inside of a tin can.

Tavenner said, "Please state your name for the record."

"Terry Thompson," Mom answered loud and clear. She sat with her back and shoulders straight. I could tell she was ready to fight.

The attorney asked if she worked at Goody's Bakery and where she lived. Then he covered his mouth, whispering to Moulder and Velde. They talked for a moment; then the lawyer said, "You're dismissed from this hearing."

Mom sat for a moment, looking at the attorney.

"I said, dismissed." Tavenner repeated.

She gathered up her purse and coat and the sheriff led her away.

Everything drained out of me. Here we were, ready for the worst and nothing had come of it. I should have been happy, but there was a sick feeling instead. It must be adrenalin, like the professor had said at the demonstration. It makes you feel sick after a fight.

⚖️　⚖️　⚖️

I thought about leaving and going home with Mom, but I didn't want to miss McCloud's testimony. I remembered Aunt C was at the house listening to the hearings on the radio so Mom wouldn't be alone. I sure didn't want to miss him: there was always a lot of excitement when McCloud was around; anything could happen.

Velde sent one of his young assistants to talk to the TV crew. Afterwards, a cameraman moved close to the door where the witnesses came in. He set up more lights and shone them in the direction of the entrance.

Wow, must be somebody important!

Chairman Moulder banged his gavel and announced, "The Committee is back in session. We call the next witness, Archibald McCloud."

Archibald? That's his first name? No wonder he always goes by McCloud! He's never going to hear the end of this!

The door opened and McCloud was escorted in by the sheriff. They stood in the open doorway for a moment, staring into the lights.

"Jeez, fellas, cut the lights, will ya? You're blindin' us," McCloud complained.

The sheriff started in and tripped, catching himself.

"No kiddin'," McCloud said, "cut the lights. You, want to kill someone?"

The TV crew turned several lights away so they didn't shine directly on McCloud and the sheriff. Moulder shuffled papers and talked to Velde with his hand covering the microphone. The same Committee member who slept in his chair during Mom's and Camilla Pearl's testimony disappeared from view again as he tilted back.

While Moulder and Velde whispered, McCloud squirmed in his chair, craning his neck to see who was in the courtroom. He spotted me and winked.

After he was sworn in, Moulder asked, "What is your occupation?"

"I'm a dogger and setter."

"A what?"

"I work in a sawmill. I'm a dogger and setter."

The senator looked over his notes, whispering to Velde. He forgot to cover the microphone, and we heard him say, "Isn't he the president of a lumber workers local?" The other Committee members nodded in agreement.

Moulder wiped his forehead, turning back to McCloud. "Mr. McCloud, please state correctly, for the record, your occupation."

"For the third time," McCloud began.

"Answer the question!"

"Dogger and setter!"

Moulder snarled, "Mr. McCloud, I can hold you in contempt!"

"For being a dogger and setter?"

The audience snickered. Moulder banged his gavel and glared at the crowd. He wiped sweat from his forehead and sighed. "You are an officer in a union, are you not?"

"I am."

"Why didn't you say that?"

"You asked my occupation. President of the union isn't a paid position. I work for wages at Happy Camp Sawmill. Despite the name, I'm not very happy."

The audience snickered again and Moulder banged his gavel repeatedly. "I'll clear the room," he threatened. The senator covered the microphone and talked with Velde. They whispered for several minutes and shuffled papers as heads bobbed in agreement.

"Very well, Moulder sighed, "tell us what you do in the mill. What does a dogger and setter do?" He said "dogger and setter" like he was talking about poop and vomit.

McCloud explained that a log was placed on a metal carriage resembling a railroad flat car. The log was attached to the carriage by a series of iron fasteners called "dogs." Two enormous saws tore through the log, one saw on the bottom and the other on the top. "I ride next to the log, making adjustments or setting the cut. It's not the safest job in the world."

"Humph, I think that's all we need," Moulder said, dabbing his wet forehead. "Let's move this along, Mr. McCloud." In a loud voice, speaking slowly, as if talking to a child, he asked, "Are you now, or have you ever been, a member of the Communist Party?"

"I cannot answer that question...."

"Cannot or will not?"

"Let me explain - it's not a simple answer."

"Answer the question! Yes or no! Are-you-now-or-have-you-ever-been-a-member-of-the-Comm-u-nist-Par-ty?"

"I want to...."

"Yes or no?"

"But...."

"Mr. McCloud, do you have contempt for this committee?"

"Mr. Chairman, I do have contempt for...."

He didn't have a chance to finish. There was a bright flash and explosion.

All around me, people were yelling and taking cover. The sleeping Committee member kicked his feet in the air, falling to the floor, leather chair and all. The rest of The Committee dove under the table.

I stood rooted to the floor, watching. The scene resembled the time Red and I were at the demonstration and the riot broke out; everything was in slow motion. Someone was talking softly near me. I looked down and there was a guy from KZAM by my feet.

"I don't care, break in on the commercial! 'Duz, does everything' can go to hell, dammit; we need to go live! This is an emergency...." He spoke in a hushed voice into the mike, "The hearing room is in confusion - there was an explosion - origin unknown - everyone has taken cover, including your reporter. This is happening at this very moment...."

One of the TV cameramen tried to calm the crowd. "It's only a TV light," he said, but his voice was soft and no one heard.

McCloud, who was used to speaking from the floor at union meetings, stood up, his voice roaring through the room, "Don't worry, Senators, no one's shooting at you! Just a TV light blew up!"

One by one The Committee members peered out from under the table.

"Ducked under those tables pretty quick! Ya look pretty nervous," Mc-Cloud said.

The radio commentator made his way to McCloud, holding the microphone near him.

Slowly, The Committee emerged from under the table.

"What's wrong, Senators," McCloud continued, "guilty conscience for getting people fired from their jobs with these witch hunts? Using stool-pigeons and paid liars as witnesses? Yeah, I'd hide too, if I were you!"

"Shut him up!" Velde screamed at Moulder.

"All the lynching in the south, all the people murdered…. The Committee can't find a single Klansman to prosecute! But you deport plenty of the foreign-born who refuse to be informers!"

"Shut him up! Velde screamed, grabbing the gavel from Moulder and pounding it. "Shut him up! Shut him up!"

The Committee recessed for almost an hour. During the recess I met Red in the hallway. We walked a bit to stretch our legs. When we rounded a corner, we saw the old Negro man by himself, writing furiously on a notepad. He looked at his wrist watch, then gave us a smile. "Better get back in there," he said. "It's time to start."

The gavel banged to resume order.

"This Committee is now in session," Moulder snarled. "This Committee will not tolerate outbursts! If there is one more outburst from you, Mr. McCloud, you will not have another chance to make a mockery of this hearing." Moulder sighed deeply. "Now, I will ask you one more time. Are you now, or have you ever been a member of the Communist Party?" He leaned across the table waiting for the answer. He looked like a hawk ready to pounce on his prey.

"I tried to explain. I'm not sure what you mean by being a Communist." McCloud began. "Does it mean…."

Moulder interrupted him, "Yes or no?"

"I can't…."

"You are in contempt!" Little bits of spit spewed from his mouth. "Remand him to the county jail. This Committee is adjourned!"

Two Sheriffs ushered McCloud out of the room; each holding his arm. It had all happened so fast, Red and I looked at each other open mouthed. I motioned to Red to come on and we rushed toward the door, pushing our way through the crowd. I wanted to get home as quickly as possible.

Chapter Twenty-Three

W hen Red and I returned from the hearings, we found Mom and Aunt C in the kitchen, drinking coffee.

"There are sandwiches," Mom said, pointing to a platter.

"Tuna?" Red asked.

"Did you hear McCloud on the radio?" I asked breathlessly. "Wasn't he great?" I could hardly contain myself. What McCloud said to The Committee after the TV bulb exploded was the best thing to happen in all the hearings.

"Yes, we heard, and yes, there's tuna," Mom replied. "They broke in right in the middle of a commercial for Duz." Mom was grinning, "And yes, he was great!"

"He was good, Terry," Aunt C said sadly, "but he's in jail."

"What did they get him for?" Red asked.

"Contempt of court," Mom told us. "The defense committee's working on his bail right now." She looked worried. "We're running out of people to put up money or their homes for bail. But we did get one offer of a house."

"Who? Do I know him?" I asked.

"Did you see an old Negro man at the hearings?" Mom continued.

I nodded.

"I hoped he made it to the hearings. He's the one that put up his house as collateral for the bail bondsman."

"No kidding? I had him pegged for an old goat herder."

"Goat herder? Josie! That was Reginald Stacks, founder of the Free Press Herald, one of the oldest Negro newspapers in the country. You just called one of the best writers a goat herder!"

My face felt hot. "Well, I guess you really can't tell anything by a person's looks," I said hiding my embarrassment. I changed the subject. "Speaking of looks, there was a woman there wearing a hat with a pheasant feather in it. Was she your friend that got the passes for us to get into the hearings?"

"Doesn't sound like her. She isn't the type that stands out."

"You should have seen Red, he looked like a real reporter, pencil behind his ear, press pass in his hat - really cool."

"The reporters were cool guys," Red added. I took notes and the union asked me to write up the story, for real. In fact, I gotta take off, I want to work on it."

"Take some sandwiches with you," Mom offered. "You're still a growing boy," she said, poking him in the ribs.

He picked up three sandwiches. Mom wrapped them in wax paper and put them in a paper bag.

⚖   ⚖   ⚖

In the evening, we gathered around the TV to catch Charles Herring's Early Edition News, hoping to see pictures from the hearings. The first story was about the hearings. They told it from the point of view of how the TV crew felt about their camera light blowing up and causing confusion. They apologized a lot. There were pictures of McCloud talking, but no sound. I was so ticked off. I wanted everyone in the world to hear what he said!

Terry pointed out a woman they were interviewing. "Isn't that the woman with the hat?" she asked. "The one with the pheasant feather?"

"Yes," I replied. We moved closer to the screen.

"My name is Brenda Hart," the lady with the hat told the reporter. "I speak for all God-fearing Americans and patriots. The scene created today was shameful."

She insinuated that, somehow, McCloud was responsible for the light blowing up. Later we discovered she was a paid witness. She was one of many traveling across the country for The Committee.

"Boy, you really can't judge a person by their looks," I said, surprised and a bit confused.

Aunt C didn't say much during the newscast; she sat on the couch sipping a drink. Looking sad, she pushed the ice cubes around with a finger. After the news finished, I asked her what was wrong.

"I'm worried about McCloud. I told him to be careful."

"But, Celeste, what choice do any of us have?" Mom asked. "Unless we lay down and play dead."

"No one ever listens to me," Aunt C said, swirling the ice and staring into her drink.

"He did what was right," Mom insisted.

"That's what Victor would have done and he would have been the one in jail."

"That's ridiculous," Mom answered.

"It would have been something; he would have found a way to denounce The Committee," Aunt C argued.

"What do you want from McCloud?" Mom asked. "Did you want him to play it close to the vest?"

"Terry, those people - The Committee - they're serious," Aunt C said, almost whispering.

"I'm proud of McCloud," Mom told her.

"I am too," I added. "He's the best."

"Nobody ever listens." Aunt C went to her bedroom, taking a drink with her.

"If you laid off the liquor, you might feel better," Mom said under her breath.

Chapter Twenty-Four

The next morning, I found Aunt C in the painting room. She was working on a new picture.

"What's up?" I asked.

She wiped the side of her hand across her forehead to push back hair from her eyes. She had a brush loaded with red paint clutched between her fingers. "I want to get this picture finished, so it'll dry in time."

"Nice one." It was a scene of an old lady sweeping leaves from a sidewalk. There were a couple of little kids playing in the background. Bright yellows, oranges and reddish browns. It looked cheery.

"What's it for?" I asked.

"Fundraiser for McCloud. I told the defense committee they could auction it off. But now, I'm kind of sorry. I'm rather fond of it."

"Why don't you bid on it yourself?"

"How conceited would that be?"

"Get someone else to do it, if you're worried what people will think."

"I just might."

"Hey! You have to hear this," Mom called from the front room. "Hurry!"

We rushed to find out what was going on, on the TV. Mom turned up the volume and we heard the announcer say, "We are at the connector on the floating bridge. A service vehicle is bringing up a car that careened off the bridge into Lake Washington early this morning. Witnesses to the event said the car was traveling at a high rate of speed. The car was identified as a 1952 black Buick, Rocket 88."

"Wow, look at that," I said as we watched a dark car being pulled from the lake, water dripping out as it was hauled into the air and transferred to the bridge. The commentator was advising listeners who lived on the east side of the lake that the bridge would be closed for at least the rest of the day. Commuters should plan on a long commute around the lake to get home.

"All we know at this point is that the car is a Buick Rocket 88," the announcer repeated. "We have the name of the owner, but information is not released at this time, pending notification of next of kin."

"They must mean there is someone inside. Hey, you know who has a car like that? Doctor Harmon," I said.

Mom and Aunt C both looked at me.

"He does," I said. "I heard that FBI agent Brock talking to Harmon about driving a big car, a Rocket 88. He said it was as big as a B-17."

They looked skeptical.

"Probably a coincidence," I shrugged. We listened to the news in the evening, but there was no information on who may have been in the car when it went into the lake.

⚖ ⚖ ⚖

The next morning I went to fetch the newspaper, and the green Chevy was parked under the madrona tree. The hair on the back of my neck stood straight up. Why in blazes were they back?

"Mom, Aunt C, we got company again."

Mom looked out of the window and pulled the shade. "Ignore them. They came early this morning."

"Does Aunt C know the FBI is back?"

"Not yet, she's sleeping late."

Mom gave me the funnies as she headed into the kitchen with the rest of the paper. I remembered Uncle Victor used to say, "The funnies aren't funny anymore...." Before I even got to Blondie and Dagwood, Mom came bursting through the double doors, waving the paper.

"Josie, I guess you were right after all."

She pushed the paper in front of me, pointing to an article. The headline read: *Accident on Floating Bridge. A local physician, Doctor Carlton Harmon died yesterday when his car plummeted off the connector of the floating bridge. Witnesses said the car, a Buick Rocket 88 was traveling at a high rate of speed. The authorities speculated the driver lost control. There have been many accidents at that point on the bridge since it opened for traffic in 1940.*

"Mom, what's Aunt C gonna say? She worships Harmon."

Chapter Twenty-Five

Mom went to pick up McCloud when he was released from jail. It had taken weeks to arrange the bond for his bail. Mom and Aunt C thought there was skulduggery involved. Mr. Stacks, owner of the Free Press Herald, had signed papers putting his house up for bond, but every time they went to get the papers for McCloud's release, the bail bondsman asked for more signatures and more proof of ownership of the property. Finally, the bail bondsman called telling her the papers were ready.

Aunt C was painting in the laundry room when there was a loud knock on the front door.

Two women waited on the porch. One was short, shorter than she appeared in the brochure in Harmon's office. Mrs. Harmon, Katherine Harmon, looked very different in real life. She couldn't have been five foot tall. She had straight black hair and violet eyes, eyes like the movie star Elizabeth Taylor.

"Hi, I'm Kat - Katherine Harmon," she announced. "Is Mrs. Jenkins home?"

I was so surprised to see the doctor's wife on our porch, I forgot my manners. I stood staring at them before I remembered to invite them in to the living room.

The woman with Mrs. Harmon was tall. She clutched a purse to her bosom and kept looking around like she was afraid she might be seen.

The taller woman looked familiar, but I couldn't place her. She kept her eyes on the doctor's wife. I left them seated in the living room while I went to find Aunt C.

Aunt C was sitting in a straight-backed chair with newspapers spread around her, sanding a Masonite board covered with gesso. Bits of white powder were on her lap and covered her hands. It seemed like a lot of work when you could buy a canvas at an art supply store; but she explained you couldn't buy anything like the boards she prepared for painting. She painted in tempera. "I get more detail and it dries more quickly," she always explained.

"Aunt C, you aren't gonna believe who's in the front room."

"What's wrong?" she asked, jittery.

"It's okay," I assured her. "It's Harmon's wife." I said it quietly, almost hissing her name, so the two in the front room wouldn't hear. "There's another woman with her."

Aunt C blinked a couple of times. "Harmon's wife? Doctor Harmon's wife?" She put down the gesso board and sandpaper and went to wash. She smoothed her hair with her hands.

"How do I look?" she asked, tucking her shirt in her jeans.

"You look great, let's go." I was anxious to know why Doctor Harmon's wife and her sidekick had appeared out of the blue.

When we got to the front room, Mrs. Harmon rose from her seat, extending her hand to Aunt C. "Katherine Harmon - Kat," she said. She turned to the other woman, "Perhaps you remember my husband's nurse, Miss Smyth?"

I hadn't recognized her without her white uniform and lime-green sweater. Still, she looked all business even though she tried to smile.

Aunt C offered them something to drink, but Mrs. Harmon said they had come on business and it wouldn't take long. She stared at her hands clasped in her lap and seemed to be searching for words. Finally she said, "First, I want to tell you how very sorry I am about your husband's passing."

"That goes for me as well," Aunt C said quietly.

"Yes," Katherine Harmon said, their eyes met. "This is a bad time, for both of us. I wanted you to know my husband had great respect for your husband." She looked away from Aunt C. "And a great deal of guilt, I think. Things were done - I know he was deeply ashamed." She spoke so quietly, I had to lean close to hear. "He was being coerced by some powerful people. I'm not saying the things he did were justified, only that there were reasons. He confessed to me that he violated the right to privacy, and medical care was interfered with...."

She looked like she might cry, and stopped for a moment to compose herself. "I believe Carl would have wanted me to apologize to you. In some way, I feel both men were victims. My husband was under a great deal of pressure. I believe it caused the accident, made him lose control of the car and plunge into the lake."

While Mrs. Harmon spoke, Aunt C listened with her head bowed. There were tears in her eyes.

"I just wanted you to know," Katherine Harmon said, rising to her feet. "Anything he did that may have been detrimental to you or to your husband was done under duress."

Aunt C didn't speak. She was crying softly. Finally, she said, "I know it was difficult for you to come here."

"Thank you for listening to me," Mrs. Harmon said. "There is another reason we came. The folder, please, Miss Smyth."

The nurse took a manila envelope from her purse. It had been folded, crinkled and crushed into a small space. She handed the envelope to Aunt C. "Please read this after we're gone," Nurse Smyth requested. "Doctor asked me to give this to you and only you, if something happened to him. I've had a devil of a time delivering it. The federal agents pawed through everything in the office. They visited my home, but they didn't find it. Every time I tried to bring it, the agents were parked in front of your house."

Aunt C accepted the envelope and walked with them to the door. They were half-way down the front steps when I remembered something.

"Wait," I said, stopping them. "Mrs. Harmon, what about your son? What happens to him, without your husband?" I remembered Agent Brock threatening Harmon with jail, saying his wife and their son would end up on welfare.

"Davey? He has Cerebral Palsy, but he's doing well," she assured me. "Doctor was concerned about his son above all other things. He carried a huge insurance policy to cover Davey's medical expenses. But thank you for asking. That was very considerate."

I watched the two women make their way down the sidewalk to their car, when the agent's green Chevy appeared. It slowed when they came along-side Mrs. Harmon and Nurse Smyth. I guess they figured out they had already delivered the envelope because the car did a U-turn and drove away.

Nurse Smyth held one arm as she made a fist and brought her arm up quickly to her chest. It was a move I had seen in a foreign movie; Mom said it was the European version of the middle-finger salute.

Good old Nurse Smyth. You just never know how people are going to act.

When I came back to the house, Aunt C was on the couch shaking her head. "Unbelievable," she said. "Totally unbelievable."

"What, the visit from Mrs. Harmon?"

"It was like a voice from the dead," she continued. "I knew Doctor Harmon was a good man."

I thought about it for a while, but I wasn't convinced. A good person? Maybe. It seemed to me he was trapped - a son with Cerebral Palsy. Maybe he did things he didn't want to do. I still had doubts about the pills he was giving Aunt C. How far would he have gone if he hadn't driven into the lake? I wasn't glad he had an accident, but I was relieved. Aunt C couldn't get another doctor to give her a prescription for more "happy pills." She was getting better. Doing more art work, and was more cheerful. As Mom said, Aunt C still had too many drinks after supper, but she was definitely better.

Aunt C clutched the crumpled manila envelope Nurse Smyth had given her.

"Aunt C, what's in the envelope? Aren't you dying to know why the Feds wanted it so badly?"

She handed it to me. "You open it."

It was sealed tightly. I ripped the top open. Inside there were three typed pages and one piece of typing paper folded up. I took them out and spread them on my lap.

Chapter Twenty-Six

"Man oh man, a real cup of coffee," McCloud said, plopping down in the Morris chair and taking a sip. He had spent weeks in jail before enough bail was collected. There were dozens of people being investigated and subpoenaed by The Committee. Mom said money for legal expenses was really tight.

McCloud's clothes were rumpled and smelled of cigarettes.

"You can use the shower. Your clothes and things are still in the spare room," Mom told him.

"Hey, skinny, did ya miss me?" McCloud asked me.

"Did you miss us?" I countered.

"Oh, heck no. I loved the goofy guy I shared a cell with."

"What was it like, in the can?" I asked.

"Let him alone, Josie," Mom chided. "The man has to get his breath."

"It's fine," he grinned. "The food and lodging? Lousy. There were plenty of smokes. People traded cigarettes for things and used them to gamble on cards. I played enough pinochle and poker for cigarettes and matchsticks to last a lifetime."

"Your clothes smell like you won a lot," Mom commented.

"I got a good poker face," he said to Mom, "I learned it from you." He winked at me.

"What were the other prisoners like?" I asked. "In junior high we went on a field trip to the County City Building. They took us on a tour of the jail. It was embarrassing. It reminded me of the zoo, when I saw all those guys behind bars."

"It is kind of a zoo," he said, "the way prisoners are treated, without respect."

"What were the prisoners like?"

"Interesting. Some shouldn't have been there at all."

"Like you?"

He nodded. "Pretty clear in my case, not so much for some of the other cats. Some needed a head doc. A couple were vets from World War Two who seemed shell-shocked. There were some hard cases too."

"Hard cases?"

"Second-story men, professional crooks, and a couple of guys that got kicks out of beating up women."

"Yuck. Were you able to stay away from them?"

"Everybody did; the guards had to keep the woman-beaters away from the rest of us."

"What else? Was it boring?"

"Josie, maybe he'd like to hear our news," Aunt C said, coming into the living room. She gave him a big hug. "Let me get the envelope," she said, going to her bedroom.

When she returned, she handed the manila envelope to McCloud, and told him Harmon's wife Katherine and Nurse Smyth had appeared one day at our door.

"Take a look," she urged.

McCloud removed the contents, three typed sheets of paper and a small folded paper. He read aloud as Mom looked over his shoulder. "John Robertson, M.D., Medical Office, King County Medical Examiner."

"Jeez," McCloud said, "this is the coroner's report."

"Look at the date," Mom pointed out. "That's only a couple of days after Victor died."

"I knew it!" McCloud said. "I bet Harmon had the report all the time."

"I don't think he had a choice," Aunt C answered.

"Harmon could have gone to the pen for a long time," McCloud said, "Josie heard the Feds threatening him with jail for insurance fraud. Let me read the rest. Hmm, I don't get a lot of this medical jargon. It might as well be in another language."

"Go to the bottom of the last page," Mom said, "where it says cause of death."

"Thrombosis," McCloud said. "Death from natural causes. Thrombosis? That's a stroke, isn't it?"

Mom nodded. "Well, at least we know now."

"You know what also makes sense," McCloud said, "I bet the FBI made Harmon hold the report back. The agents wanted people to think Victor committed suicide. It demoralized everybody, even us, but we didn't believe it. It had a huge effect on the union. There was a lot of in-fighting; it was hard to get the members together to negotiate their contract. It's just the kind of crap the FBI does best, cloak-and-dagger stuff, dirty tricks."

"Look at the small folded sheet of paper. What do you make of it?" Aunt C asked.

There were two words typed on the paper: Truly sorry. There was no signature.

"What do you think it means?" I asked.

He asked Aunt C, "You said Harmon left instructions this be sent to you, in case anything happened to him?"

Aunt C nodded.

"I think Doctor Harmon was asking forgiveness," McCloud said.

"But how could he know he was going to have an accident?" I asked.

"What if he planned it?" McCloud answered.

⚖ ⚖ ⚖

I thought about it for a long time and it made perfect sense. The agents were threatening to send Doctor Harmon to jail. They black-mailed him, making him do things he didn't want to do. Things he hated. Maybe the doctor thought going off the floating bridge was his only choice. His wife and son got insurance money from the accident. He was finally free of the agents. But still, what did they want him to do that was so bad he had to commit suicide?

Brock threaten Harmon, he wanted him to drug a patient. Harmon said he wouldn't do it. I got a shiver. What if they wanted him to give something bad to Aunt C, something worse than the happy pills? I wouldn't put it past them. I guess that would be the last straw for a doctor.

Now that Harmon was gone, we would never know. At least we did know the truth about Uncle Victor's death. Just as I always thought, my Uncle Victor would never commit suicide. He was the bravest, best man there ever was.

Chapter Twenty-Seven

When Alain had called me from New York, he told me to expect a package from his mother and a letter from him. He didn't want the Navy to read his letter, so he mailed it while he was in port. I ran to the mailbox, every day. The package and the letter arrived on the same day.

Three silk scarves tumbled out of the package: one gray, one black and the third the brightest scarlet I had ever seen. They were real silk, from Paris. I held mine up to the light and a rose appeared. The silk was as soft as baby powder.

Mom, Aunt C and I put on the scarves and paraded around the house, singing. Wearing them, made us giddy and we did little dances. When we finished prancing and exclaiming over our gifts, I excused myself and went to read Alain's letter in private.

My Dear Jozette:

It was wonderful to hear your voice. You have been on my mind since I left Seattle. Our tour this time was one of many adventures. I told you we encountered weather on the way from the islands to

New York. The weather consisted of gale-force winds, around 47 knots for two days. That would be about 50 miles per hour. We left Haiti earlier than scheduled to take the ship out to sea because of the storm. I won't go into all the details of life on board ship during a storm, only there was much work and little rest.

The storm was, in a way, the climax of an event that had begun the moment we docked at Port au Prince. When we arrived, there was a strike, workers refusing to load and unload ships. Our captain ordered us to unload one particular ship, saying it was necessary for French security, highly unusual for the commander to do this. We were never able to discover the nature of the cargo. Several of us who were members of unions talked with other crew members. We felt we could not in good conscience become strike breakers, no matter what the commander ordered. Some sailors outright refused to work the ship, while many more became "sick" or participated in a slowdown. The result was the struck ship was never unloaded and the storm arrived, forcing us to leave. I wasn't able to find out how the strike ended. But our captain was very angry and several of us may have charges against us. I am unsure of what this means, but the talk is that there may be a trial. The leaders could spend time in the brig or even face dismissal from the service. I would not like to spend time in jail, but I wouldn't feel too bad if I was put out of the service before my term is up.

I am mailing this from a post office in New York City so it won't be read by the officers if I were to send it through regular naval channels. Please write and tell me how things are with you. How did your friend Mr. McCloud fare during The Committee hearings? I hope he is not in jail. What about your mom and Aunt Celeste, are they feeling better? Have you returned to school? I look forward to hearing from you,
Much love, Alain

I re-read Alain's letter a zillion times. After I practically memorized it, I went to find Mom and tell her what he had written. I found her and Goldie in the living room. He had just returned from his organizing trip for the union. They were standing in front of the fireplace, and he had his arms around her.

"I don't care," Mom said.

"But Josie, how will she take it?"

"How will I take what?" I demanded.

"Why don't we all sit down?" Mom suggested. She and Goldie sat across from me, holding hands.

"Goldie got subpoenaed," she said.

"What? I thought all that was over!"

"Not by a long shot," Goldie said, "The powers-that-be hate the union, and everything we stand for."

"There's more, Joz," Mom continued. "We're getting married. We've talked about it for a long time and Goldie finally got his divorce."

"When?" I stuttered.

"He thinks we should wait because of the hearings, but we've waited long enough."

"Josie, how do you feel about it?" Goldie asked. "We won't do anything you don't want."

I didn't answer right away, I wanted to say the right thing. Finally I told them, "It's okay with me; you guys are the ones getting married, not me. There is one thing though...."

"And that is?" Goldie asked.

"Do I have to live with Rocky? He gets on my nerves."

Goldie laughed out loud. "He said the same thing, about you."

"What! He knew about this first?"

"Sibling rivalry already," Mom smiled.

They really looked happy, and they deserved it.

"I guess it wouldn't be so bad if Rocky came over on a holiday, once in a while." And it wouldn't hurt to have a bigger brother around, when things got dicey at school. Even one that isn't crazy about you. Family comes in handy.

Chapter Twenty-Eight

With all that happened in the past few months, I hadn't seen much of my ace, Jennie Boggs. I went to her house vowing to see her more often. When I knocked on the door, her mom hollered to come in. She was at the kitchen table peeling potatoes.

Mrs. Boggs was a large woman, with a wide nose and mouth. Her lips parted showing her teeth. It wasn't a smile, it was more like a grimace. Her blonde hair was pasted to her forehead and sweat poured down her face.

"Hi, Mrs. Boggs."

She motioned for me to sit, but I stood in the doorway. "Is Jennie here? Haven't seen her for ages."

"She's staying in the International District, over on Jackson Street."

When I asked her address, she said, "You know the Safeway Store on Jackson? She got an apartment two doors down, up the stairs, first floor; it's the one on the right."

My stomach was churning as I waited for the bus to the International District. Her own mother didn't know her address. How could a kid my age afford an apartment? Jennie didn't get along with her mom and had talked about living with her dad, in Montana; but this was a big surprise.

A few weeks before, a couple of girls from high school had stopped me to talk about Jennie. One of them asked, in a snotty way, "Where's that red-headed friend of yours?"

I stared at her, not answering.

"We heard she's staying with some man," she added. Then the other one butted in. "Maybe she's having a baby...."

"And maybe you don't know what you're talking about," I answered and hurried away. There was always lots of gossip and rumors about kids at school, so I forgot about it.

⚖️   ⚖️   ⚖️

At the second doorway down from the Safeway I found a steep set of steps that looked like they went to apartments. When I knocked on the door her mother had indicated, there was no answer; so I ripped out a page of ruled notebook paper and left a note, which slipped neatly under the door.

Jennie called me the next day. It was great to hear her voice.

"Don't go anywhere Jennie, I'm coming right over."

⚖️   ⚖️   ⚖️

This time, there was an answer when I knocked. I stepped into a big living room with an old couch and a few chairs scattered around. Jennie sat surrounded by a pile of boxes, taking out china plates from one. We hugged.

"Boy, am I glad to see you!"

"Me, too." She smiled, but somehow she looked sad. Her face was puffy, and she had gained some weight.

"What's happening? How did you manage this place?"

"Lee Sparrow, my boyfriend, the one I told you about...."

"Your boyfriend from grade school?"

151

"He's out of the Army." In almost a whisper she added, "We're married." She held up her hand and the light caught the ring on her left hand.

"Married? And you didn't tell me?"

"Your uncle had just passed on...."

"Is your mom okay with you getting married?"

She held up one of the plates she was unpacking. "China," she said, "with real gold."

Each plate had a golden ring around the border.

"Jennie, your mom agreed?"

"That's why we did it right away, so she wouldn't change her mind."

Nothing felt right, or sounded right. She wouldn't look at me when she talked.

"When can I meet this famous Lee Sparrow?"

"He's at work now."

"You okay Jen? You look kinda peaked."

"I'm going to have a baby," she said softly. She got up to move one of the boxes. I could see her belly - it was big.

"When?"

"Four more months, December."

"Wow. You excited?"

"Been looking at baby names," she said, producing a small book. "I like Benjamin."

"Nice."

"My dad's name."

We talked about names from the baby book until she said it was time to start supper. I took the hint, and left for home.

"See you soon?"

"Soon," she answered.

"I really missed you."

She smiled that sad smile again.

Nothing Jennie had said added up. She wasn't yet sixteen; there was no way she could get married. According to my calculations, she would have gotten pregnant way before her Lee Sparrow was in the picture. She must have gotten pregnant around the time I met Alain. I was beginning to wonder if there was such a person as Lee Sparrow, the one she said was her "one and only true love." She insisted that going out with other guys was just for fun; it wasn't serious. She looked so scared when I left, I wanted to cry.

She had taught me how to do all the new dances, to do the Bop and Stroll. Because she had a good sense of humor, was funny, cute, and had bright red hair, she always had a lot of boys around. Most of my other friends were more serious, and I could probably say they were more responsible. When Jen and I went places together, I felt free.

⚖ ⚖ ⚖

The next time I went to Jennie's place, a man answered the door and told me she had moved. He didn't know where so I went to her mom's house. When I got there, it was empty too.

Mom never told me who I could have as friends. She didn't say anything about Jennie, but I knew she didn't approve. She called her "the butterfly girl." For a long time I didn't tell her that Jennie was married and having a baby.

One night, I had a dream about her. One minute she was doing the Bop, and the next she was getting fatter and fatter and fatter until she was the size of her mother. Her lovely red, almost orange hair faded into blonde. It was Mrs. Boggs. She smiled and showed her teeth.

Chapter Twenty-Nine

T he French Navy "invited" Alain to leave the service early. He was being punished because he and other sailors had refused to unload a ship on
strike in Haiti. Alain didn't protest when he got the discharge papers six
months earlier than expected. He wrote he was leaving Paris to work in
Vancouver, Canada. I got that pitty-pat feeling. Was he moving to Canada
to be near to me?

⚖ ⚖ ⚖

"Mom, are you sure you don't want to go?"

Alain had come down for the weekend. He, Red and his new girlfriend,
Frieda, were in town, too. We decided to head back up north to Vancouver
to see a movie. Not just any movie, but one that had been spirited into
Canada from the U.S. We were on our way to see *Salt of the Earth*, a movie
the-powers-that-be in the U.S. had moved heaven and earth to keep from

being made or to be seen once it was finished. Uncle Victor's paper wrote about the problems making the movie. Goldie told us the Mine Mill and Smelter Workers Union was having a preview showing to advertise it and raise money.

The story was about a miners' strike in Southwest U.S. While it was being filmed, the actors and crew were shot at and the lead of the film, Rosaura Revueltas, a movie star from Mexico, was deported.

The union organizer portrayed in the film was a real person. Like Uncle Victor, he was being investigated by The Committee and might get ten years in jail.

⚖️ ⚖️ ⚖️

"Are you sure, Mom?"

"No, honey, you and Alain go on; I've got plans. McCloud's coming down."

"What's up with him? Haven't seen him in ages."

"He's coming to see the lawyer about the appeal."

"It's taking long enough."

"He says it will be years before the State Supreme Court makes a decision."

"What are you going do? Sit around playing pinochle or Scrabble?"

"Goldie and I might go out...listen to some music with Celeste and McCloud."

"At the Blue Moon?"

"No. There's a new club opening off Jackson Street. One of Celeste's friends works there."

"A musician?"

"An artist, Bill Much. He does caricatures and charges a couple bucks a pop for them."

"What kind of music?"

"Jazz. Oscar Holden and one of his sons, David are playing. Do you know him?"

"He went to Garfield High School. Real nice guy."

"The club's different: apple crates for tables, sawdust on the floor. The drinks are served in fruit jars."

⚖️ ⚖️ ⚖️

We made the trip to Canada in Red's car because it was new, a Chevy, or as some call it, a "shove it or leave it." It seemed like a good idea to take Red's car when we crossed the border. He had a Washington State Driver's License and Alain's was international, which might raise some alarms with the border guards. Not that he was doing anything wrong; we just didn't want to be held up on our way to see the film.

Alain was born in New York and spoke English because he went to school in the U.S. and Canada. He had a U.S. passport. But then he also had a French and a Canadian passport because of his mother. He was the only person I knew that had citizenship in three countries.

Every time we crossed the border, I felt guilty. I'm not sure where the feeling came from, maybe it's because there were so many uniformed guards at the border and they always asked questions like they suspected you of something. Maybe it was the way they looked. They didn't exactly greet you with a big grin that said, "Let's be friends."

When we got to Blaine, we drove through the American side without stopping and lined up for the border guards from the Canadian side. They asked each of us where we were born, as they listened for accents to discover if we were aliens sneaking into the country. "Why are you visiting Canada?" a guard with a walrus mustache asked.

We didn't tell him we were on our way to see a blacklisted pro-union movie.

"Pleasure trip," Red told him.

The old walrus waved us through and we were on our way. Soon we passed the sign to Port Roberts, a town built on a spit of land belonging to the U.S. You had to go through Canada to get there, unless you went by boat or airplane. It's the most northwest part of the U.S.

⚖　⚖　⚖

It began to snow.

"Wow, look at that," Red said.

Large flakes fell on the windshield and melted. Then it stopped. I rolled the window down a crack. You could smell snow in the air.

"It's really cold," I said, shivering.

"Maybe we'll get snowed in," Frieda said, hopefully. She explained she grew up in Minnesota. "We get snow every winter. Doesn't seem the same without it."

We got to the outskirts of Vancouver and easily found the theater, near the University of British Columbia. There was a line-up outside for tickets, but we didn't have to wait. Alain's mother, Tamara, stood by the door waving her arms, tickets in hand. When Alain decided to look for work in Canada, she had followed him.

This was my first time meeting her. I was surprised how short she was. Her gray hair peeked out from under a black beret and she wore a scarlet silk scarf around her neck like the one she had sent to me. She looked like a cook. She was a little plump with rosy cheeks and smelled like cinnamon.

The theater was packed. Before the movie started, a representative from the Mine Mill Union spoke to the crowd, explaining the background to the movie, *Salt of the Earth*, and asked people to protest the U.S. government blacklisting the movie.

The lights dimmed, and the story began. It was the first time I had seen a movie where women were the important characters. The wives of the striking miners had a special kind of oppression. They were treated as the servants in the family; but when the strike started and the men couldn't picket because of an injunction, the women took over!

After the film, Alain and Tamara spoke with the man from the miners' union that introduced the movie. He hugged Tamara and shook Alain's hand.

"Thanks for doing this," he told Alain.

We said goodbye to Tamara and piled into Red's Chevy. Once we were on the highway, Alain told us he was offered a job working with the Miners' Union. The man he had spoken with after the film was an old friend of his father.

"Working for the Miners' Union, that's exciting," Red said. "What would you do?"

"The union's getting ready for a strike against a big copper mine in the Okanagan, near the U.S. border. They think it's gonna be a tough one. I'd be working for the International and with the Women's Auxiliary."

"Strange combination," Red remarked.

"Not really," Alain told him. "The Women's Auxiliary has a history of supporting the men. Once, they rescued a defunct local when the men gave up. They were demoralized, but when the auxiliary kept fighting they got their spirit back. Sort of like the movie."

"I'd be writing and translating in French for the newspaper. Also, I can travel back and forth across the border more easily than some of the more well-known union members. We can coordinate with the American locals

- until I get pegged," he laughed. "The guy I spoke with said there were RC-MP's (Royal Canadian Mounted Police) spying during the movie. They've been spying on students at the University of British Columbia."

"The job means I'll be seeing you guys a lot," Alain said. He leaned over and whispered to me, "Especially one certain person."

We were almost out of Vancouver when the snow started coming down hard. A car driving toward us slid and almost hit us.

"Bet it's a woman driver," Red said, and Alain laughed.

"Boy, you guys didn't learn anything from that movie, did you?" I snapped.

There was a dead silence before both Red and Alain agreed I was right.

"I don't see anything wrong with it," Frieda said.

I guess men aren't the only ones who can be chauvinistic.

⚖ ⚖ ⚖

Before long a white blanket covered everything. The car heater was going full-blast and Red was doing a great job of keeping us on the road, out of the ditches. The snow made the world look new.

We started singing. We sing everywhere we go. If we are traveling, at meetings, parties, strikes, sad or happy, everything is an excuse to sing. My favorite is *Goodnight Irene*.

Last Saturday night, I got married
Me and my wife settled down
Now me and my wife are parted
Gonna take another stroll downtown
Irene goodnight, Irene goodnight
Goodnight Irene, Goodnight Irene
I'll GET you in my dreams

I insisted we sing Leadbelly's version - *I'll GET YOU* in my dreams, not *I'll SEE YOU* in my dreams. It's how I feel. I don't like waiting for change. I want to make things happen, to make a better world, the way Uncle Victor would have wanted.

REAL TIME LINE & DEFINITIONS

78 Records: Ten-to-twelve inch vinyl discs recorded at 78-80 rpm.

B-17: Boeing built airplane, the B-17 Flying Fortress was introduced in 1938.

Apartheid in South Africa: 1946 African Mine Workers are paid twelve times less than their white counterparts and are forced to do the most dangerous jobs. Over 75,000 Africans go on strike in support of higher wages. Police use violence to force the unarmed workers back to their jobs. Over 1.000 workers are injured or killed. (Source: Student hand-out U.N. Cyberschool bus). 1948 Policy of Apartheid (Separateness) adopted when Nation Party (NP) takes power. 1950 Population classified by race. Group Areas Act passed to segregate blacks and whites. Communist Party banned. ANC (African National Congress) responds with campaign of civil disobedience led by Nelson Mandela. (Source: BBC News Africa, South African Profile—online.) 1952 Abolition of Passes and Coordination of Documents Law. This misleadingly named law requires all Africans to carry their passports. (Source: Africanhistoryabout.com)

B.Buck "Butterball" Ritchey: Country music DJ on KVI from 1943-1965.

Blue Moon tavern: See the University of Washington History Link for more information.

Bob "Bop" Summerise: Pioneering African-American DJ and owner of World of Music Record Shop located on Jackson Street, Seattle Washington. (Source: Northwest Music Archives.)

Bolshevik: A member of the political party that led the Russia in 1917.

Bop-Lindy Hop: One of the first types of bop style dancing.

Camel Walk: A free style dance, later called the Stroll.

Cannery Worker's and Farm Laborer's Union: A Filipino-led union, became Local 37 ILWU, the International Longshore and Warehousemen's Union. (Source: Seattle Civil Rights and Labor History Project, University of Washington – online.)

Canwell: Albert F. Canwell (1907-2002) was a Republican Washington State legislator from Spokane, Washington, who served one term in the House from 1946 to 1948. He was chairman of the Canwell Committee, officially titled the Legislative Joint Fact-Finding Committee on Un-American Activities in Washington State, which sought out Communists and other "subversives" during the "Red Scare" era. Canwell, who had worked various jobs, including farmworker, freelance journalist, and police photographer, campaigned for the House seat on an anti-communist platform. He helped write the resolution establishing his committee. Canwell chaired both of the committee's hearings in 1948 that targeted alleged Communist influence in the state's labor movement and at the University of Washington. Three UW professors were fired as a result of the committee's work. Canwell ran for office many times afterward but never won another race. He was one of the defendants in the sensational John Goldmark libel suit in 1963. He ran his own "intelligence service" in Spokane, Washington for decades and continued to gather information on people and groups he deemed subversive. He died, unrepentant and unapologetic, in Spokane in 2002. (Source: University of Washington History Link Essay 9887.)

CRC: Civil Rights Congress, formed in 1946. The Civil Rights Congress was formed in the late 1940s with the merger of three organizations: the International Labor Defense, the National Federation for Constitutional Liberties, and the National Negro Congress. The organization brought worldwide attention to racism in the United States by presenting a petition to the United Nations titled We Charge Genocide. The petition was presented by Paul Robeson and William Patterson. (See Wikipedia for more information.)

DAR: Daughters of the American Revolution, founded in 1890, a genealogical society open to women who prove lineal descent from a patriot of the American Revolution.

Dave Beck: International President of the Teamster's Union until the early 1960s when he was convicted and sent to prison for corruption. (Source: University of Washington History Link) Beck was loved by the Chamber of Commerce and called a "sell-out" by militant unions and many of his own members.

Fa. Coughlin: Roman Catholic priest; anti-Semite, anti-Communist and anti-Socialist, pro-fascist. (Source: Wikipedia.)

Ferlinghetti: Lawrence Ferlinghetti, poet, painter and co-founder of City Lights Booksellers and Publishers in San Francisco. He is best known as the author of A Coney Island of the Mind. Urban myth recounts many well known authors as having paid homage to poetry and independent thought by visiting the Blue Moon tavern in Seattle. If Mr. Ferlinghetti did, it is likely to have been in the 1960s. (Source: University of Washington History Link for more information on the Blue Moon tavern.)

Freddie Steele: 1912-1984 Boxer.

French-Indo China: A part of the French colonial empire that included Vietnam, Cambodia and Laos until 1954. (Source: Wikipedia.)

Frizzell: Lefty Frizzell, 1928-1975, was a prolific songwriter. He had four songs in the Country Top Ten at the same time in 1951. (Source: Wikipedia.)

Garfield High School: A public high school located in the Central District of Seattle, Washington. Several notable musicians attended the school, including Jimi Hendrix, Quincy Jones and Ernestine Anderson. (Source: Wikipedia.)

Green Death: Ale made by the Seattle Rainier Brewing company in the 1950s and '60s. (Source: SFGate "Green Death Malt Liquor for SF Beer Week," Lessley Anderson, February 8, 2013.)

Goodby Pork Pie Hat: A jazz standard composed by Charles Mingus in 1959 as an elegy for saxophonist Lester Young. It was later renamed Theme for Lester Young. (Source: Wikipedia)

Hispaniola: Island in the Caribbean.

Holden: Oscar Holden is often called the "Father of Seattle Jazz." His son, Ron, a vocalist hit the Billboard Charts in the 1950s with Love You So. His son, Dave, was a jazz musician. (Source: University of Washington History Link)

Honky Tonk'n: The correct name is If You Got the Money Iv'e Got the Time, by Lefty Frizzel. A prolific songwriter, Frizzell had four songs in the Country Top Ten at the same time in 1951. (Source: Wikipedia)

House Un-American Activities Committee: The first hearings were held in Seattle in 1948.

Interstate Highway System: Enacted in 1956.

Kangaroo Court: A mock court in which the principles of law and justice are disregarded. (Source: Wikipedia)

Kerouac, Jack: Novelist and poet. He was often referred to as the "King of the beat generation." Author of On the Road. All his books are in print today (Source: Wikipedia) Urban myth recounts many well known authors as having paid homage to poetry and independent thought by visiting the Blue Moon tavern in Seattle. If Mr. Kerourac did, it is likely to have been in the 1960s. (See the University of Washington History Link for more Information on the Blue Moon tavern.)

KKK: The Ku Klux Klan with its long history of violence, is the most infamous and oldest of American hate groups. Although black Americans have typically been the Klan's primary target, it also has attacked Jews,

Latinos, immigrants, gays and lesbians and Catholics. Over the years, since its formation in December 1865, the Klan has typically seen itself as a Christian organization, although in modern times Klan groups are motivated by a variety of theological and political ideologies. (Source: Southern Poverty Law Center)

KVI: Leading country music station in Western Washington until the 1960s.

KZAM: an FM station that began broadcasting in 1961.

May Day: (International Worker's Day) began in Chicago in 1886 as a movement for the eight-hour day. It is one of the most celebrated holidays around the world.

Moulder: Representative Morgan M. Moulder, Democrat from Missouri's 11th District.

NATO: North Atlantic Treaty Organization.

Pike Place Market: The Pike Place Market was created in 1907. In the 1930s the area beneath the Main Market's neon sign and clock became a free speech corner to Socialists, Communists, Evangelists, Technocrats and just plain crackpots. Japanese American farmers sold produce in approximately 4/5 of the market stalls until World War Two started. (Source: Walt Crowley, University of Washington History Link.)

Peach Arch Park: Located at Blaine, Washington, the park straddles the International Boundary between the United States and Canada.

Peekskill Riots 1949: August 1949, the KKK, American Legion and other right wing groups attacked concert goers at a Paul Robeson concert to raise money for the Civil Rights Congress. Thirteen people were injured and the event was canceled. In September the concert was held with thousands of people present and some 2,500 trade unionists forming a human wall to protect Robeson as he sang. People were attacked leaving the concert. Many were seriously injured. (See: History Today The Peekskill Riots, 1949. Volume 62, issue 4 2012.) (Also see: Peekskill's days of infamy, by Steve Courtney, The Reporter Dispatch, September 5, 1982.)

Polio (Poliomyelitis): Often called Infantile Paralysis, epidemics were regular events in the developed world, primarily in cities during the summer months. There were major out-breaks in the 1940s and 1950s.

Red Squad: Police intelligence units that specialized in infiltrating, conducting counter-measures and gathering intelligence on political and social groups. (Source: Wikipedia.)

Robeson, Paul Robeson b. 1898 d.1976 was an African American international star, famous for his bass-baritone voice. He was not only a concert singer but also a Shakespearean trained actor. In his youth he excelled at football, basketball, baseball and field and track. He was a Phi Beta Kappa, a lawyer and a linguist. Robeson became a spokesman for the world's poor and disposed; the most outspoken voice exposing racism in the U.S. and fascism abroad. He embraced the Soviet Union, socialism and struggles for national liberation. For this he was ostracized, blacklisted, investigated, hounded and not allowed to travel outside the U.S. which destroyed his career as singer and actor. Robeson talking about the Peekskill riot: "I'm going to sing wherever people want me to sing, and I won't be frightened by crosses burning in Peekskill or anywhere else." (Source: Brief biography Bay Area Paul Robeson Committee—online.) The Spanish Civil War stopped for a few hours while Robeson sang on January 23, 1938.

Rocket 88: The Oldsmobile Rocket 88 with a V-8 engine was made by General Motors; it was a fast car winning many NASCAR divisions. (Source: Wikipedia.)

Rosenbergs: Ethel and Julius Rosenberg were convicted of conspiracy to commit espionage. They were found guilty of passing information about the atomic bomb to the Russians. They were executed on June 19, 1953. (Source: The Guardian, June 20, 1953. "Execution of the Rosenbergs.") The Rosenbergs were arrested at the height of the McCarthyite witch-hunt against Communists. (Source: "The trial of Ethel and Julius Rosenberg" by Elizabeth Schulte. International Socialist Review, May to June 2003.) Despite massive, world-wide protest, Ethel and Julius Rosenberg were executed on June 19, 1953 at Sing Sing Prison in Ossinging, N.Y. (Source: The Rosenberg Fund for Children.)

Selectric: IBM introduced the Selectric-type ball typewriter in 1952.

Sixty-Four-Dollar Question: CBS radio quiz show 1941-1948.

Spanish Civil War: During the Spanish Civil War, (1936-39) almost forty thousand men and women from fifty-two countries, including 2,800 Americans, traveled to Spain to join the International Brigades to help fight against fascism. The U.S. volunteers served in various units (medical, combat and transportation) and came to be known collectively as the Abraham Lincoln Brigade. (Source: albavolunteers.com.)

Sap: Also known as a blackjack, is a piece of lead or other metal wrapped with leather. It is used to inflict damage to an individual without breaking the skin.

Swing: West Coast Swing is a stylistic version of the Lindy Hop.

Taft-Hartley Act: (Labor Management Relation Act of 1947) A law drafted by employers to infringe on worker's rights and curtail union activity. (Source: The Nadar Page, The Taft-Hartley Act, by Ralph Nadar, July 18, 2002.)

Tavenner: Frank Tavenner, counsel for the House Un-American Activities Committee. (Source: University of Virginia Law School 1952-1954.)

Velde: Representative Harold Himmel Velde was a Republican Congressman from Illinois. He headed the House Un-American Activities Committee in the 1950s. He was named to the House committee largely because of his FBI service as an expert on sabotage and counter espionage during World War Two. (Source: Ex-Representative Harold Velde; led Anti-Communist Unit – Times Wire Service September 8, 1985.)

VFW: Veterans of Foreign Wars.

⚖   ⚖   ⚖